BAD MEMORIES

AN UNCANNY INK STORY

DAVID BUSSELL
M.V. STOTT

BECOME AN INSIDER

Sign up and receive **FREE UNCANNY KINGDOM BOOKS**. Also, be the **FIRST** to hear about **NEW RELEASES** and **SPECIAL OFFERS** in the **UNCANNY KINGDOM** universe. Just visit:

WWW.UNCANNYKINGDOM.COM

BAD
MEMORIES

1

Look, I'm not really one for therapy, okay? If you ask me, the healthiest way to deal with your crippling psychological issues and dank self-loathing is to drink plenty of alcohol, have bad sex with stupid strangers, and spend most of your days in mortal peril. Trust me, do that and the voices in your head that keep telling you what a sack of shit you are won't get a look in.

Hey, it works for me.

Well, *works* might be a bit of a stretch.

Okay, so it doesn't work at all, but lying to yourself is Number 1 on the Erin Banks Healthy Living Top Tips List, right next to getting a pedicure and taking a relaxing bubble bath.

Anyway, this is all a roundabout way of saying that the last place you'd expect to find me is stretched out on a therapist's couch, thoughtfully sifting through the wreckage that is my life. And yet there I was, legs up, head back, and staring at the ceiling while Dr William Gourt MD, qualified Cognitive Behavioural Therapist, sat quietly in his armchair.

'Oof, where to start, Doc?' I asked, lacing my fingers

behind my head and crossing one leg over the other. 'I suppose you could say me and my parents have issues. Actually, "issues" is underselling it a touch. Calling what we have "issues" is like calling a three-day-old corpse "a bit run down".'

I shifted on the couch as I stared up at a little patch of damp on the office ceiling.

'Me and Mum, that's the real pistols at dawn stuff. That bitch does not like me at all, and believe me, the feeling is more than mutual. I actually killed her recently. Well, not *kill*-kill. Turned out it was a lookalike pulled out of my memories by a half-demon trying to drive me to suicide.' I shrugged. 'It's a whole thing.'

I turned my head to look at Dr Gourt, who continued to sit patiently in his leather armchair, saying nothing.

'Huh. Thought all that demon and murder talk might have gotten a peep out of you, but that's a classic shrink tactic, I suppose. Let the patient talk and talk, get all their crazy out. Textbook stuff.'

I went back to studying the damp patch on the ceiling. It was shaped a bit like the spaceship from *Star Trek*. My dad had always liked that show. I frowned and got back to talking.

'I'm going to save you a shit-tonne of time here and straight-up tell you the root of all my problems, Doc. My baby brother, James. He was kidnapped. Kidnapped and never given back, and my parents—my mum especially—blames me for it. Which, you know, fair dos, I had been left to babysit the kid, but how was I to know a talking pig and a bloke with glowing red eyes were going to snatch him?' I let forth a long, bitter sigh. 'Anyway, that's the night that opened my eyes to a secret world of monsters and magic, and led to me becoming a supernaturally enhanced assassin.'

I turned to the shrink again. Still nothing. I carried on.

'If you want to know what I think—and this is my non-professional opinion here—I'd say James' abduction turned me into a thrill-seeking, shallow bitch with a semi-death-wish and an inability to love or be loved. So what do you think, Doc? Am I a lost cause?'

I rolled onto my side to face the doctor, whose eyes bulged from his head like a pair of doorknobs. Not because he was shocked, but because I'd strangled him to death a half hour previous.

Yup.

Doctor William Gourt's fat tongue lolled dumbly from his mouth, his throat ringed with a livid necklace of my fingerprints.

'You know, Doc,' I said, shaking my head, 'for two hundred quid an hour, I really don't feel like you're pulling your weight here.'

I stood up from the couch. I had work to do. I patted myself down for a knife, but the sheath I carried under my jacket was empty.

'Bloody hell, Banks,' I muttered, 'total amateur hour.'

I looked down at the duffel bag lying on the ground – the one I'd brought along to carry away Gourt's head. How was I meant to remove the good doctor's noggin without my knife? I scanned the cluttered office looking for a cutting device of some kind, until my eyes landed on a letter opener sat on the doctor's desk. 'Guess this will have to do,' I said, scooping it up and examining its disappointingly dull edge under one of those antique green glass desk lamps.

Without ceremony, I jammed the pewter blade into the doctor's neck and began sawing. It was a messy job. *Really* messy. Still, it's amazing what you can achieve when you employ a bit of elbow grease and really put your mind to it. I mean, come on, who would have thought sawing a man's head off with a letter opener was even possible? Someone should have pinned a medal on me, really. Still, you try telling that to the blokes who pushed open the door to Doctor Gourt's office and found me drenched in blood, carrying a human head, and singing *Whistle While You Work*.

The two men stepped into the room, one blonde, the other a redhead, both fuck ugly. Which was unusual, given that they were incubi, a race of Uncanny that were ordinarily possessed of extremely good looks. Oh well, every litter has its runts, I suppose.

'Howdy, guys,' I said as I lobbed the severed head of their brother across the room at them.

The blonde one caught it before dropping it to the floor with a shocked yelp.

These two were on my hit list, too, but I hadn't expected to be dispatching them so soon. Having them all there in one room was a real time saver, a definite stroke of luck. I made a mental note to buy a lottery ticket ASAP.

The blonde-haired incubus threw aside a flap of his coat to reveal a samurai sword, which he drew and slapped in his palm like a disgruntled policeman.

I eyed the katana blade and sighed. 'Where were you five minutes ago?' I asked, holding up the teeny letter opener I'd been forced to hack the doctor's head off with.

'Who sent you?' growled the wannabe Highlander.

'Who do you think?'

The pair looked at each other. 'I told you Madame Ambrose would find out,' hissed the redhead.

I'll get to Ambrose in a bit. First off, I should explain what an incubus is. An incubus is the male form of succubus. They're subservient to their female counterparts, and much less powerful. Like their dominant sisters, they feast on emotions, though unlike the creatures from folklore that you might be familiar with, certain rules prevent them from sucking the life out of their victims while they're asleep. Rules agreed by the greater succubi family and the London Coven. Rules that, if broken, could lead to all-out war.

Originally, this trio of incubi had coloured inside of the lines. Instead of creeping into the homes of innocents and draining them dry, they came up with a clever plan: set themselves up as a psychiatry practice, attract a wealth of troubled patients, and feast all day on the emotional baggage of their diseased minds. It was a good deal for everyone involved. The three incubi were able to eat without harming anyone, and were actually good at their jobs by all accounts. Think of it as a sort of demonic Deliveroo where the food comes to you and the delivery driver goes home better off, too.

Thing is, the trio got greedy. So many juicy emotions, so many raw outpourings, and still it wasn't enough to sate them. Soon enough, they started to sneak into their clients' homes at night and feast on them the old-fashioned way, turning more than one poor sucker into a dried-out husk.

This was a big no-no as far as Madame Ambrose, the head of the Brighton incubus chapter, was concerned. Ambrose runs the Pink Pearl, a brothel where kinky Johns pay for the company of an Uncanny creature of their choice (or so they're led to believe). Ambrose doesn't like to think of himself as a flesh-peddler or a whoremonger, but rather a purveyor of erotic fancies. You might have noticed that I referred to Madame Ambrose as a "him" there. It's complicated. While Ambrose was undoubtedly born male (he'd be a succubus otherwise), he dresses with way too much flair to be a man, and has hair twice as nice as mine. Quite honestly, I'm not sure what I'm supposed to do with the gender pronoun as far as Ambrose is concerned, so let's step away from that nest of vipers and return to the action. All you need to know is that Madame Ambrose is a chic old queen who took exception to this trio of goons drawing trouble to his door, and hired me to get rid of them before the London Coven got wind of their dastardly deeds.

The two incubi took another step towards me, scoping me out, moving to flank me.

I tossed the letter opener and picked up the duffel bag. 'I've got room in here for three heads. You guys in?'

They hissed and did something really kinda disgusting: they opened up their faces. No, you did not misread that. The skin on their faces split like the lines of a crucifix, and the flesh peeled back to reveal huge, gaping mouths lined with hundreds of sharp, little teeth.

'I'm not gonna sugar coat this, fellers, you weren't much to look at before, but you are a right pair of eye crimes now.'

They surged towards me, one of them swinging his sword, the other raking the air with hands that had now turned into vicious claws.

My tattoos glowed bright red as magic soaked into them, making me faster, stronger, more agile. Blondie reached me first, swinging his sword in a wide arc. A wide, *sloppy* arc. Evidently, the guy hadn't spent much time at the dojo, because I was able to duck his attack, grab him by the wrist, and relieve him of his weapon with next to no effort.

'A little off the top?' I asked as I swung his own sword at him, its blade passing through his neck like he was made of marshmallow.

The redhead recoiled as his brother's decapitated head

landed at his feet, its wide-open jaws still flapping and twitching.

'Oopsie,' I said, 'that rug is definitely going to stain.'

Red lashed out, catching me in the jaw and connecting with such force that he sent me crashing over the desk. The antique lamp smashed down by my side, narrowly missing my head. I looked up to see Red standing on the desktop, looming over me and glaring down with his off-brand Predator-face.

'Sorry about turning your brothers into a stack of obituaries,' I said. 'I get carried away, and the next thing I know I'm on a real kill streak.'

Red crouched, ready to pounce, his face peeled back like the petals of some evil tropical flower. Wasting no time, I swung the sword up and relieved him of his legs below the knees. He collapsed, screeching like twisted metal, and knocked the wind from my lungs as he landed on top of me. With a mixture of fury and agony, Red's hands met my throat, his jaws snapping ever closer, eager to chew the flesh from my face.

'Sorry,' I grunted, 'I never snog on a first date.'

Magic flowed into my arms, filling up my muscles. I used the extra strength to throw Red off me, sending him sailing over the desk and into a wall decorated with all manner of medical certificates. 'Actually, that's not true,' I admitted. 'I've done way dirtier stuff on a first date than snog. I mean, *way* dirtier.'

I rounded the desk to find Red pushing himself backwards, leaving behind a slug trail of blood from his leg stumps.

I snatched one of his chopped-off limbs from the desk and held it up by its ankle. 'I think you're a little past legging it, mate.'

I tossed the severed appendage to one side and strolled towards Red, twirling the sword as I went, enjoying the moment.

His face closed up so it looked human again. 'Please... p-please... I have money.'

'Hey, me too! I'm getting, like, five grand a head for this gig. Also, don't tell your mate, but I'm definitely running out on the bill I owe him for our session, so that's money in the bank, too. Ain't I a rotter?'

Red went to plead again, but the sword passing through his neck cut him off. I mean, literally cut him off. Ha. Jokes.

I planted the tip of the sword in the floor and looked around the room at the various, scattered remains of the three dead incubi.

'Hm.'

Usually, I'd feel elated at a job well done—basking in the aftermath of another deadly fight that I'd stepped away from unscathed—but this time was different. This time my mind was elsewhere. This time I was thinking about the Red-Eyed Man, the man who stole my baby brother, and how close I was to finally finding him.

Finding him and killing him.

2

————

'Did somebody order three severed heads in a duffel bag?' I asked, as I half-walked, half-danced down the steps of Black Cat Ink.

I tossed the bloody bag at Parker's feet, where it landed with a satisfying squelch.

'Someone's in a good mood,' said Parker, stopping the bag with his toe as it slid towards him across the parlour's chequerboard floor.

'You know me, Parks, I'm always happy when I'm hitting my targets.' I touched my arse with my finger and made a hissing sound. 'Little assassin humour for you, there.'

'Very clever,' he sighed.

I rubbed my hands together. 'Three dead monsters, money in my pocket, and it isn't even lunchtime yet. I'm getting shit done, son.' I shucked off my jacket, t-shirt, and bra, and settled into Parker's reclining chair. 'Come on then, ink boy, momma needs a top up.'

Parker raised an eyebrow and snorted as he stashed the bag of heads behind the counter and took up his place next to me. He lowered himself onto his stool, his fingers stroking the tattoo gun he used to graft magic to my flesh. 'I take it you're so perky 'cos your chubby little sneak friend found those boys you were looking for?'

'Yup,' I replied. 'Cupid tracked down the place they're working out of, which means I'm about ready to tie a ribbon on this thing.'

Parker frowned. 'I'm happy for you.'

'Then tell your face that.'

'The path you're on could take you to someplace real bad. Scratch that, there ain't no "could" about it. Whatever happens, whatever's waiting for you out there, it ain't nothing but awful and worse.'

I wanted to be annoyed at him for raining on my parade, but I couldn't. Parker was right. The thing I was looking for —revenge on the person responsible for abducting my brother—was just as likely to lead to my sticky, very dead end as it was to giving me any sense of closure (which I guess is a kind of closure, but not exactly the one I had in mind).

Since Cupid crashed my vacation with news of the abductor and some ancient prophecy he was mixed up in, I'd tried to focus on the good. On the fact that, at long last, I had a lead on someone who knew of the mysterious Red-Eyed Man. The piece of shit who took James from me. Finally, after years of hitting dead ends and chasing my tail, I felt like I was close to discovering the truth. But like Parker said, the idea of any of this turning out well, of me skipping across the horizon to some Happily Ever After... well, it seemed unlikely, to say the least.

But that didn't matter.

James' kidnap destroyed my life and moulded me into what I was. A killer, detached from the workaday world, detached from everyday morals. I'd made myself into this thing, forced myself into this world, all for one reason: to make the Red-Eyed Man pay for what he did. And no matter what happened to me, I was getting that much.

'I know what I'm doing, Parks,' I insisted. 'Don't worry about me.'

'You a tough bitch, I know.'

'Tough as they come.'

'Tough still hurts. Tough still dies.'

'Just get on with it, will you?' I said, shaking my arm at him, showing him the burned out tattoos that so desperately needed an oil change.

'You sure about this?' asked Parker. 'Your tan ain't even faded yet and you're already throwing yourself into another ruckus.'

'I'm sure,' I said, giving him a playful dig in the shoulder to cement my argument.

Parker chuckled grimly then fired up his tattoo gun. Pure, white magic seeped from the blank orbits of his sightless eyes, and went travelling down his dark-skinned arm. The tendrils of light coiled around his bicep like vines around a tree, moving slowly towards the needle he held steady in his muscular hand.

Here we go again...

My muscles tensed as the metal spike bit into my flesh, sending a familiar jolt of pain up my arm that lanced through my head and into my brain. I winced and clenched my jaw shut, hard enough that I felt a tooth crack. Not to worry – the new tattoos would soon take care of that. Would soon repair the damage and make me whole again.

Parker worked in silence for a while before he spoke again. 'Do you remember the first job I got you, girl?'

I forced a smile as I took a walk down memory lane.

'Yeah, Big Alex. Heroin dealer who got pissed off that his rival was using a werewolf to fuck up his shipments.'

'Yep. Man, that wolf tore his crew up like confetti.'

'What's your point, Parks?' I asked, biting down on the pain.

'Point's this: I told you the job and you was all pumped up, certain you could handle the big dog.' He laughed. 'You always had tickets on yourself.'

'Hey, I put the big dog down, didn't I?'

'He kicked the shit out of you.'

'Only a little bit.'

'He broke half the bones in your body.'

'He should have broken the other half if he didn't want to get dead.'

Parker's sprig of dreads danced as he threw back his head and laughed. I couldn't help but join in. It's odd what you find funny when you've been in this world as long as we have. Then again, what's funnier than a friend getting hurt? That's just one of those universal things that everyone can agree on, like pizza being tasty, and Jason Statham being a hot slab of throbbing man meat.

Parker talked over the buzz of the needle. 'You were lucky that shifter didn't know your ink put you back together, otherwise he would have made sure you was dead instead of leaving you to rot behind a bin.'

'Yeah, lucky me.'

'You always been lucky in this game, girl. I mean, you found me, didn't you?' Parker flashed his big, white teeth at me.

I rolled my eyes, but he was right. Finding myself in front of his parlour when I was fifteen, defenceless, full of rage and confusion, was the best thing that could have happened to me. The way I was going—the hornets' nests I was poking at—I'd have been dead before I reached my next birthday if it weren't for his ink.

The stabbing sensation stopped as Parker took his foot off the tattoo pedal and leaned back, frowning.

'What?'

'Nothing. Just... I hope you find what you're after, girl. Hope it don't... hope it don't break you, 'cause you're right. You are tough. Toughest I ever worked with.'

'Oh, Parks, you're gonna make me blush,' I said, fluttering my eyelashes sarcastically.

'But you more than that. More than tough. More than someone on my payroll. You're my friend, Erin.'

A strange sensation washed over me. I tried to reciprocate, to tell Parker that the feeling was mutual, but my mouth wouldn't form the words. No matter how hard I tried, my lips stayed locked tighter than an uncooked mussel.

Parker offered an awkward smile and put a hand on my shoulder. 'That's all right, girl. Just don't be dead next time I see you, okay?'

'I'll... um, do my best,' I said, wincing for a different reason now.

Parker bowed his head. 'I made it weird, didn't I?'

I nodded.

He got back to work. 'Okay then, let's never do that again.'

'I was gonna say...'

'Once a lifetime was more than enough.'

'I think my heart just grew three sizes, Parks.'

He jabbed down harder with the needle, making me flinch. 'Fuck you, girl.'

The sky was black, and there was a cold, unforgiving lick to the air.

I was positioned on the rooftop of an office block, crouched behind an air-con unit and using a pair of binoculars to spy on a window across the road. Behind the window was a private office, within which a meeting was scheduled to take place. A meeting I had a vested interest in.

Snooping from a distance was a marked departure from my usual way of doing business. I've been described as many things—a sledgehammer, a bulldozer, a flaming wrecking ball covered in dog shit—but rarely, if ever, have I been called subtle. This particular occasion called for some finesse, though, because this wasn't just a job to me. There was more at stake here than relieving some dodgy shrinks of their heads and collecting a pay cheque. Way more. I couldn't risk anything going wrong on this one. Couldn't risk losing my lead, losing my advantage, so there I was, skulking around in the middle of the night and spying on a window like a lovelorn ex.

I needed to see what this meeting was about before I made myself known to the people involved. Before I challenged them face-to-face. That was the trick. Do the recon, gather the intel, and only when I knew what I was walking into would I step out of the shadows and start busting noses.

'I'm freezing my nuts off here,' grumbled the fat cherub sat by my side, munching on a cheese and pickle sandwich.

Despite appearances, the cherub was a good pal of mine. We'd known each other a long time, long enough that I have all sorts of affectionate nicknames for the guy: Tiny, Chubby Bubby, Little Angel, Butterball, That Fucker. Mostly, though, I just call him by his given name...

'You know, Cupid, maybe you wouldn't be so cold if you wore more than just a nappy.'

'Don't have much room for a wardrobe,' he replied. 'Bit light on storage solutions under the pier.'

'You also don't need to live under a pier like a weird fucking hobo. You earn enough off me. Get yourself a proper place.'

He griped some more and took another bite of his sandwich, spilling crumbs everywhere.

Fact was, Cupid was never able to hold on to money for long. No sooner had he wrapped his fat little mitts around the stuff than he was handing it over for booze, or passing it to the cashier of his favourite casino.

'I like the pier,' he said. 'I like being close to the sea. It's soothing.'

'Then stop your bellyaching,' I told him. 'I'm working here.'

I peered through the binoculars and felt my heart quicken as I saw my target pass in front of the window I was spying on. There he was: Chad Bowles, five-seven, about 70-80 kilos. He had a crop of brown curly hair and a muscular build, but wasn't exactly what you'd call buff. His lips were thin and his nose ran to a sharp point. He wore jeans over a pair of combat boots, and still had his bomber jacket on, like he wasn't planning on staying indoors long.

'Is that all the thanks I get?' huffed Cupid. 'I bring you this lead out of the kindness of me own heart, and what do you do? Call me a hobo and question my fashion choices?'

I looked down on him (and I mean that in every sense of the phrase). 'I've said thank you, like, ten times.'

'Once, actually.'

'Well, pretend I said it another nine times after that,

then. Anyway, I paid you, didn't I – isn't that thanks enough? And who paid for your dinner?'

He posted the last of the cheese and pickle sandwich in his mouth and let out a terrific burp.

I slapped the top of his bald head. 'This is meant to be a covert mission, you grubby little bastard.'

'Well, excuse me all to fuck.'

I shook my head at him, then returned to the binoculars and trained them on the window. Thankfully, it seemed my target hadn't heard Cupid's belch, or possibly mistook it for the rumbling of an oncoming train, or maybe one of the trumpets of the apocalypse.

Long before we'd arrived on the rooftop, Cupid had explained that he'd caught the person I was watching discussing the Red-Eyed Man. Apparently, he'd overheard Chad chatting while he was busy at the roulette wheel, talking in hushed tones about some ancient prophecy. That was three days ago. Since then, I'd asked Cupes to gather any info he could on the man while I took care of the incubi gig. Like I say, I didn't want to stumble into this thing half-cocked, so for seventy-two hours I'd been like a kid on Christmas Eve, desperate for the clock to speed up so I could get to unwrapping my presents. Still, I stayed strong. Patience is a virtue, or so I've been told.

'You're sure you heard right?' I asked Cupid. 'You're sure this rendezvous has something to do with the guy who took my brother?'

'Unless you know some other bloke with red eyes who hangs around with a talking pig.'

I wasn't expecting the Red-Eyed man to show up to the meeting in person, but learning about another member of his little cabal was reason enough to be there. Maybe this third party would be the stepping stone I needed. Maybe Chad was the one who'd finally lead me to the big bad.

'And they definitely didn't say what this prophecy was about?' I asked.

'Of course they did,' replied Cupid, 'I just thought I'd hold back that vital piece of information 'cos I've got no fucking clue what I'm doing.'

I gave him the kind of look that left a mark. 'You realise I could drop kick you off this roof right now, yeah?'

'Sure, and I could flutter into your flat while you're asleep and take a nice, hot dump in your mouth.'

Not wishing to test the filthy little bugger any further, I brought my eyes to the binoculars and aimed them across the street. I saw a flicker of activity through the window and adjusted the lenses. The target was moving, heading to the office door as if to answer it.

'Shut up a second,' I hissed. I leaned forward, gripping the goggles tight. 'Looks like we're on.'

Cupid shielded his eyes against the moonlight and squinted to get a better look. 'About bloody time.'

Chad Bowles opened the door to greet his visitor. The person who may well have proven to be the key to the mystery surrounding James' abduction.

'What the...?' I gasped.

My heart fell into my stomach. Ice filled my veins. I knew the person.

Actually, *knew* him was a bit of an understatement.

'Kirklander?'

3

My head felt like it was about to cave in on itself. Kirklander. Always fucking Kirklander.

Cupid fluttered his wings and took to the sky, but before he could get away from me, I grabbed him by one of his chubby ankles. 'Stay.'

'What for?' he groused. 'I thought the plan was for me to hover outside the window with my ear cupped to the glass.'

'The plan just changed.'

I carried on watching through the binoculars as Kirklander conversed with Chad, a big, cocky grin on his face. I death-gripped the binoculars so hard I'm surprised I didn't crack the lenses. After a couple of minutes of chat, Kirklander accepted a package and tucked it into the inside pocket of his long, ivory-coloured coat. Following that, he gave a casual salute by way of a goodbye, then left the office the same way he'd arrived.

I abandoned my vantage point, raced down the building's inner stairwell and burst out onto the street. My tattoos burned hot and bright, pulsing in synch with my heartbeat as I ran, making my nerve endings throb. I took cover behind a parked car and watched as Kirklander left the building opposite, his coat snapping in the breeze like a flag cutting into a stiff crosswind. An easy whistle played on his lips as he shoved his hands into his pockets and strolled away.

What the hell was going on? Now Kirklander was involved in this? How did that make any kind of sense?

That all-too-familiar feeling of betrayal washed over me, and I had to force myself not to drop to my knees and throw up.

Cupid appeared, fluttering down from the night sky and hovering next to me at head-height. 'What are you going to do?'

'I'm going to get the truth.'

'Need a hand?'

'Go home, Cupes. This has nothing to do with you.'

I pulled out a handful of money and tossed the notes skywards as I stepped out from behind the car. Cupid bobbed around in the air, frantically grasping for cash like a dog trying to burst soap bubbles.

I headed off after Kirklander, keeping my distance, ghosting him discreetly. I didn't want to creep around; what I wanted was to run right up to that sack of shit and feel his ribs cave beneath my fists, but first I needed to see where he was going. To see who else was involved in this sick little plot.

He turned right down a side street, slipping out of view. I darted forwards so I wouldn't lose him, and peered around the corner he'd taken. He was heading towards Tarner Park. What for? Nothing in there except a few trees, a crumbling old turret, and a whole lot of graffiti, as far as I knew.

Kirklander vaulted over a locked gate without missing a step—his coat flapping out behind him like a cape—then landed like a cat and carried on walking. I glanced around for any watching eyes, and when I found none, sprinted forwards and did the same.

I touched down on the other side of the gate to see Kirklander disappearing behind the stone turret, a crumbling old folly built by some mucky muck as an observation tower back in the who knew when. I carried on after him, hugging the shadows provided by the park's long, flint wall, careful to keep my footfalls nice and light.

Kirklander had let me down a lot over the years. No, more than let me down. He'd double-crossed me, hurt me, almost gotten me killed on a couple of occasions. But nothing like this. How was he mixed up with the man who took James? Had he known what had happened to my brother all along? The idea that Kirklander had been working against me the whole time made my anger spike like a witch's hat.

I rounded the turret and found Kirklander standing still with his back to me.

'So,' he said without turning, 'are you going to join me, or are you going to carry on stalking me like a weirdo?'

Shit.

He turned, a big smile on his face. 'It's good to see you. Always good.'

'Something you want to tell me?' I asked through gritted teeth, my breath frantic and short.

'Nope.'

I began to walk forward, a tiger approaching her prey, ready to pounce, ready to bite and tear. 'You sure about that?'

Kirklander's smile faltered and his forehead creased. 'It was stupid. I know it was.'

That was it. I couldn't hold back any more. Time to put a

tag on that fucker's toe. Tattoos burning fierce and red, I charged him like a bullet train, screaming, my shoulder connecting with his chest and lifting him off his feet. I carried him backwards, down a steep, grass slope, until a molehill caused me to lose my footing and we both tumbled to the ground.

I rolled into a crouching position, Kirklander mirroring me.

'What are you—?'

I took a swing, my knuckles connecting with his cheek. His head snapped to the side, blood spraying, painting the green grass red. He keeled over and slammed into the ground, his head kicking up a clod of turf.

'Bastard!' I yelled, pouncing on him.

But he was ready. He caught me and kicked out, sending me tumbling over his body. The world did a somersault until the ground halted my journey, knocking the wind from my lungs.

'What the hell are you doing?' cried Kirklander, up on his feet, running the back of his hand across his mouth and smearing blood across his chin.

I clambered to my feet. 'You always do it. Always!'

'Do what? Is this a guessing game?'

'Whenever I think that maybe you're changing, you fuck me over.'

'Baby, I haven't got the slightest clue what you're on about.'

I wasn't interested in his words. Not yet. I wanted to hurt him first, and get answers later. I pulled out a knife.

'Whoa now, there's a line,' said Kirklander.

'Yeah. And I think you fucking crossed it.'

I ran at him, reason out the window, fuelled by blind anger. I went to stick him in the shoulder, but he twisted, caught my wrist, and cranked it hard. I yelled out in pain as I heard a couple of my carpals go crack, and felt the knife slip from my hand.

Kirklander kicked the weapon aside, sending it further down the grassy slope. 'Just stop.'

'No.'

I launched a backhand at him, lifting him off his feet and sending him corkscrewing to the ground again.

He looked up at me, shocked. 'Baby...'

I loomed over him, my fury red hot. 'I'm not your baby.' I raised a boot, ready to bring it down on his ankle. Ready to hear *his* bones pop, ready to hear him scream high and loud. Only my foot didn't come down. Instead, *I* went *up*. 'What the hell?' I thrashed around, unable to get back down, a fly caught in an invisible web.

'Will you just stop and listen for once in your life?' said Kirklander, his arm outstretched towards me as he returned to his feet.

His hand was glowing. Ribbons of bright purple magic strobed and danced as they wove around his palm and between his fingers. He was holding me up with sorcery. Lifting me off my feet and keeping me airborne. Since when had he been able to do that?

'Put me down,' I yelled, thrashing around impotently.

'I would, but since you just pulled a weapon on me, I think I might keep you there for a bit. What the fuck, Erin? A punch, fine, a headbutt, cool, but a knife?'

'You're working for them,' I screamed, ashamed as I felt my eyes start to prickle with tears

'Working for who?'

'Don't pretend. Don't pretend!'

'I swear to Christ, Buddha, and Tom Cruise himself, I have no idea what I've gone and done this time.'

I couldn't hold them back any more. Tears streamed down my cheeks. 'I know you're working for the man who took James.'

Kirklander's eyes grew wide and he took a step backwards, his arm lowering, the purple light from his hand fading. I sagged as my feet met the ground, my body limp as a marionette. I swiped away my traitorous tears.

'What did you say?' Kirklander whispered.

'Don't lie to me, Kirk. Just don't.'

'Wait a second. Can we get on the same page, please, because I am well and truly lost here.'

I stood, and as I did, Kirklander took another step back. He needn't have bothered, the fight had left me.

'Cupid found a guy connected to the Red-Eyed Man.'

'What? He did? That's great.'

'Yeah, it is. And I caught them meeting someone tonight.'

'Okay. Who?'

I said nothing.

'Oh...' said Kirklander, putting it together. 'Now, wait just a second...'

'How long have you known? Have you always been on his side, laughing at me from the sidelines?' I felt my anger rise again, my tattoos ramping up my adrenaline, leaching magic from my surroundings. My wrist was repaired already, my fist solid, strong.

'I don't know anything about the Red-Eyed Man,' said Kirklander. 'No more than the little bits you've told me, I swear.'

'I saw you with my own eyes, Kirk. Saw you in that room, meeting up with a man involved in some kind of prophecy that's meant to involve James.'

'I don't know anything about a prophecy. All I know is, a

man with money wanted me to help them find something. That's all. A search and retrieval job for a fat stack of cash, nothing more.'

I paced back and forth before him, breathing heavily, not sure whether to believe him or not. This was Kirklander, 75% of him was basically bullshit.

'How do I know you're telling the truth?'

'You don't think too highly of me, do you?' he replied.

'Should I?'

Kirklander let forth a long exhale. 'Look, if what I'm being paid to do has something to do with your brother, maybe instead of trying to stab me, you should join me so we can figure out what's going on.'

I walked over to where Kirklander had kicked my knife, and picked it up. 'If you're lying to me...'

I slipped the knife back into its sheath.

'Come on, you know I'm not. Not about this.'

I frowned and bobbed my head. Call me stupid, you wouldn't be the first, but in that moment, I was sure Kirklander was telling the truth. Something about his eyes, maybe. We'd done a lot to each other over the years, but I'd always felt like he cared about me on some level. Now my rational side had cooled the white-hot heat of my anger, I knew this was one thing he wouldn't use to fuck me over. Not James. Even Kirklander knew better than that.

'Okay,' I said. 'Fill me in.'

Kirklander raised an eyebrow and opened his mouth to reply.

'—I swear to God, if you turn that into a sex joke, I'll make you swallow your own feet.'

'Aw, you're no fun. You know, I should be the one pissed off here.'

'Um, why?'

'The knife. You were going to stab me, Erin!'

'Only in the shoulder, you big baby.'

Kirklander laughed and shook his head. 'We really are the worst, aren't we?'

'I think that's a given at this point.'

We left the park walking side-by-side.

So, Kirklander and I were working as a team again. Working together on the most important job I'd ever taken. If I was wrong about him, if he tried to double-cross me again, he'd pay for it with his life. I was playing for keeps this time. No more second chances.

4

Kirklander had been hired to locate an artefact: something that his employer, Chad Bowles, referred to simply as, "The Tenth".

In order to track down this item, Kirk had been handed some information. Not much, just a package containing a few scant historical details and a sketch of the artefact itself. He'd since passed this information along to me, the pages of which sat on my lap as I drove us to the Library of the Uncanny. I peered down at the sketch, doing my best to keep the speeding car in the correct lane, but falling foul of the occasional swerve.

'Can you please watch where you're going?' asked Kirklander, sat in the passenger seat, his foot digging around for a non-existent brake pedal. 'This is still technically my Porsche, you know?'

'Like balls it is,' I said, not taking my eye off the sketch. I still couldn't make head nor tail of the thing. 'What is it, exactly?' I asked.

'A piece of stone,' he replied, 'about the shape and size of a wand.'

'Right. *Is it* a wand?'

'Nah, this Tenth thing's supposed to be serious, and wands are for wieners. Only an end-of-the-pier magician would waggle around one of those little tiddlers. A real wizard would be mortified to be caught using a *wand*.'

'Right. Much better to lug around a massive wooden staff, eh?' I replied, referring to the macho length of lumber he liked to keep about his person.

'Exactly,' he said,

'I was being sarcastic.'

'I knew that. I did!'

The Tenth. A source of power of some sort, at least according to the information Kirk had been given. Artefacts said to hold great power seemed to be ten-a-penny in the Uncanny world, I wondered what was so special about this stone not-wand, and how it tied in to the so-called prophecy surrounding James' kidnap.

'Talking of magicians,' I said, 'want to tell me how you pulled off that little trick back at the park?'

'What little trick?'

'You held out your hand and stopped me in my tracks. You lifted me off the ground. Since when were you able to do that?'

Kirklander shifted uncomfortably in his seat. 'I've, uh, been practicing. A lot. Really getting my head down.'

I waited for the "getting my head down" bit to morph into a smutty joke, but it never happened. Which made me suspicious. It was too obvious a set-up to just leave dangling. Quite unlike Kirklander not to exploit a perfectly good double entendre. Something was up. Kirk was a minor magician at best; he had access to magic, but only in a limited capacity, and with a very loose handle. Without his staff to keep him focused, he had little to no control of the

Uncanny. The supernatural energy he absorbed would shoot out of him at all angles, firing off chaotically, bouncing off walls and injuring bystanders at random. Yet, despite all this, he had used his powers to scoop me up and hold me in the air like I was a prize in an arcade claw machine.

Something stunk.

'Since when did you have the patience for practice?' I asked.

'Hey, a guy can evolve, can't he?'

'I always took you for more of a *de*volver.'

He was keeping something from me for sure, but I decided it best not to push the matter. I'd wheedle it out of him soon enough.

'Oh, look, here we are,' said Kirklander, pointing out of the car window at the entrance to the Library of the Uncanny, expertly changing the subject. 'You know,' he continued, 'the aisles of that building are awfully secluded in places.'

'We're too busy to bang, Kirk,' I replied, pulling the battered Porsche to a stop across the road from the entrance.

'I can be very quick.'

'Yeah, I know.' I killed the engine and got out, darting across the road and ignoring the angry honks of a passing car.

Kirklander joined me at the nondescript door to the library, the letters LOTU etched into the wood above a closed peephole.

'Wait a minute,' I said, noticing something was missing, 'where *is* your staff?'

'Ah, so now you are interested in some—'

I elbowed him sharply in the ribs.

'Fair enough. Told you, been practicing. Don't need it any more.'

'Kirk, what's going—?'

He reached out and knocked on the door, causing the peephole cover to immediately slide back and reveal a familiar pair of yellow eyes. Vollard.

'What?' he barked. 'What d'you want?'

'Bit of research. Now open up, you old swine,' replied Kirklander.

Vollard's single, long, bushy eyebrow shot up. 'Mister Kirklander!'

'*Mister*?' I said, turning quizzically to my companion.

'Hey, I can charm more than just women, baby,' said Kirklander.

I stuck my fingers down my throat and gagged. Soon after, the peephole slammed shut, bolts slid open, and the door swung wide to reveal the keeper of the books in all of his tall, stooped glory. Vollard stood there, shrouded in a dark blue robe.

'Such a long time since last you were last here,' he said, putting his arm around Kirklander and ushering him inside like an old friend.

I rolled my eyes and followed.

'Been a busy bee, my lad,' Kirklander explained. 'People to kill, ladies to deflower, you know how it is.'

Vollard giggled and shook his head. 'This world could do with a few more like you, Mister Kirklander. Yes, indeed, it really could.'

'I'd say one is more than enough,' I interjected.

Vollard paused and looked over his shoulder at me through narrowed eyes. 'Hm. You're the one with the tattoos and not much else, right?'

'Okay, Judgey McJudge-face.'

Vollard snorted from his beak of a nose and continued his forward shuffle.

'Don't mind her, Vollard, mate,' said Kirklander, grinning and wrapping an arm around my shoulders. 'I've got her under my wing.'

'Remove that arm or I will. From its socket.'

'Still a bit of work to do, obviously, but we're getting there,' Kirklander noted with a twinkle.

We emerged from the narrow corridor into the huge, majestic library, its bookshelves, crafted from fine, dark wood, filled level after level, reaching skywards until I lost sight of them. Brass ladders on sliders clung to each bookcase, leading up to any shelf out of reach, then on to the next level and the next set of bookshelves, and up, and up, and up.

'What is it you're after then, hm?' asked Vollard as he eased his bent body down into the comfy leather chair sat behind his desk.

Kirklander pulled out the sketch of the artefact with a flourish, and slapped it down on Vollard's desk.

The book keeper frowned and peered at it. 'What's that, then? A wand?'

'When is it ever a wand?' said Kirklander. 'It's called The Tenth. A magic doodad I've been trying to track down.'

'The Tenth? Hm. Can't say it rings a bell,' said Vollard. 'Then again, much of the inside of my head is probably dust by this point. Chances are, half of the things I knew are gone. Curse of a long life, that.'

Seemed Kirk and I were on our own. We left Vollard at his desk and clambered up several brass ladders until we arrived at level seven, which held an extensive collection of books cataloguing Uncanny objects and artefacts. After at least two hours of pulling old, dusty book after old, dusty book from the shelves and poring over them at a reading desk, Kirklander sagged into his chair and unleashed a sigh.

'Quiet up there!' came Vollard's voice from way below.

'Like I said earlier, you've no patience,' I said, just as bored as he way, but not willing to show it.

I carried on, leafing through page after page detailing artefacts of all kinds, from a rust-coloured penny that, if slipped into a person's pocket, would kill them within the hour, to a magical axe, forged in Heaven. Which looked familiar. I wondered if that was the same axe the crazy redhead I ran into in Blackpool had been carrying.

I carried on thumbing the pages. Kirklander had given up helping me and was scrolling through his phone instead, reviewing his Uchat feed (a social media site for Uncannies that you won't know about).

'Get back to work,' I said, turning the page of the book I was reading to reveal a drawing of a hat that allegedly gave its wearer the ability to read minds.

'Okay, I'll be good,' he said, his hand disappearing under the table to place the phone in his pocket

I tensed as I felt a hand touch my knee.

'Get off of me, you dirty bastard. I told you, we don't have time.'

Kirklander's brow creased. 'You what?'

'Take it off before I break it off.'

He lifted up his arms and showed me his paws. 'My hands are clean.'

The hand under the table crept up to my thigh. Which meant Kirklander had either grown a third hand just for groping (which I wouldn't put past him), or someone else was feeling me up. I glanced down to see a pig's trotter resting on my leg.

'What the fuck?' I stood and flipped over the table to

reveal a hog looking up at me, dressed in sackcloth clothing and standing on his hind legs. 'You?'

The pig grinned, revealing a set of large, rotten teeth.

'You know this pig?' asked Kirklander. 'Weird question, that.'

'It's the one who was there the night James was taken. It is you, isn't it?'

I drew my knife and went to grab the hog. The animal snorted, sending mucus spraying from his snout, then lunged for the piece of paper that Chad had given Kirklander. The one detailing the artefact. Having snatched it, the then pig turned and ran away as fast as his little legs could carry him. Which was, apparently, very fast indeed.

'Get him,' I screamed, giving chase, Kirklander hot on my heels.

'Keep it down up there,' Vollard stage-whispered from below.

I bolted after the fleeing pig, but he waved a glowing arm and brought a bookcase down in my path, burying me under a torrent of dusty old tomes. Kirk pulled me from the literary avalanche.

'You okay?'

'I'll live,' I spluttered.

'What the bloody hell is going on up there?' came Vollard's voice.

'Pig infestation,' I shouted back as I clambered over the fallen bookcase, keeping my eyes on the pig as he ducked around a corner and out of sight.

'You break it, you pay for it!' Vollard called back.

I made it to the corner, only to find the hog stood waiting. He punched out a trotter and an invisible fist struck me in the stomach, leaving me gasping.

'You little bastard,' said Kirklander, ready to unleash

some magic of his own, only to find himself face-planting into the floor beside me.

'Thanks... for... the help,' I managed, struggling to catch my breath.

Kirklander rolled on to his back, stunned. 'I can't believe I'm fighting a pig,' he said, wiping blood from his nose, 'and the pig is kicking my arse.'

Tattoos burning bright, I hopped back to my feet, fists clenched, primed for action. The pig stood there watching, his face twisted into a smile.

'Do you know who I am?' I snarled.

A fat, pink tongue poked from the pig's wheezing mouth, and his shoulders shook. Was he laughing at me?

'What did you do with my brother?' I demanded. 'Tell me!'

I took a step back as the pig began to float into the air.

'Careful,' said Kirklander, reaching out to pull me back. I shrugged him off and moved forward.

'Tell me where James is!'

The pig clapped its trotters together and the wall behind him exploded, showering the library with bricks and dust and leaving a gaping hole to the outside.

'The prophecy,' grunted the pig.

'What bloody prophecy? Why are you doing this?'

'Too late,' said the pig. 'We won. Father is coming.' The pig twisted around as though turned by invisible hands, then shot forward, through the hole and away. I darted after him but it was too late. As I looked outside, the pig disappeared from view, carried away in a ball of strobing red magic.

'Shit. Shit!' I cried, picking up a brick and launching it at speed, cracking one of the bookcases.

The pig. At last. Finally, I'd crossed paths with someone connected to the kidnap. And I'd let him get away.

Vollard shuffled into view, his tiny eyes opened unnaturally wide as he took in the destruction around us.

'She did it,' said Kirklander.

***

As I drove us back into town, heading for Black Cat Ink, I felt a strange mixture of elation and frustration.

The artefact that Kirklander had been hired to find was definitely connected to James, to the Red-Eyed Man, to whatever the mystical prophecy was that surrounded the whole thing. I was getting closer. After all these years of frustration, the mystery was starting to open up. I didn't have sight of the whole picture yet, though, and I'd let one of the few creatures who could show it to me get away.

'I've never seen Vollard that angry,' said Kirklander, sulking in the passenger seat.

'Thanks, uh, for paying for the damages.'

'No problem,' replied Kirklander, in a way that told me it was very much a problem. 'So then... a magic pig.'

I nodded. 'Yup.'

'I mean, you've mentioned him before, but still. Not the sort of thing you come across every day, even in our weird world.'

'Yeah, I can't say I've ever met any other magic pigs. And believe me, I've looked.'

'So what now?' asked Kirklander. 'We lost the info.'

'What does that matter? We know what it said, we know what the artefact looks like, and we know that the pig and the Red-Eyed Man are after it, too.'

Kirklander's brow furrowed. 'Didn't you say I was accidentally working for the Red-Eyed Man? Why would they give me info on The Tenth, just to snatch it back?'

It was a good question. 'Maybe they saw that I'd found out what you were doing for them, and didn't like the idea of me jumping on board.'

'Little do they know how stubborn you are.'

'Exactly. We're going to carry on looking for this notwand, and we're going to start by meeting up with the bloke that hired you. Either this Chad Bowles bloke gives us some dirt freely, or I'll beat it out of him. Maybe I'll kill him either way. Why not, I could use some cheering up.'

'Sounds like a plan. I'd like to go a second round with that pig, too. Little fucker loosened a tooth.'

I pulled to a stop outside Black Cat Ink and hopped out of the Porsche, feeling energised, feeling purposeful. After all of that searching, all of that rooting around in the dark, finally a face was beginning to cohere. A lifetime spent hunting the Red-Eyed Man, and now here he was, almost in my sights. I was close. Pretty soon I'd have my revenge on the man who stole my brother and capsized my life. I'd kill him, boogie in his blood, and rip out the piece of shrapnel he left in my brain the day he took James.

I pushed open the shop door and tap danced down the short flight of stairs leading to the tattoo parlour, Kirklander close behind.

'Hey, Parker, guess which little piggy me and this idiot bumped into?'

I was parting the beaded curtain at the bottom of the steps when I realised something was off. I stopped and held out an arm, holding Kirklander back.

'What is it?' he asked.

I licked my lips. 'Blood,' I replied, tasting a familiar,

coppery tang in the back of my mouth. 'Parker?' I said warily. 'You in?'

After all my years as a killer, I'd developed a feel for it. For death. It hung heavy in a room. Hung heavy in *this* room, in Parker's parlour. Someone had died here, and recently.

I scanned the area and saw nothing out of the ordinary, save for Parker's absence. Then Kirklander touched my arm and pointed. A pair of black boots stuck out from behind the shop counter on the far wall. I recognised those boots.

I walked forwards in a daze, knowing what I was about to see, knowing that I wanted to stop and not look. If I didn't look, it might not be true.

I looked.

Behind the counter, twisted and bloodied and dead, was Parker. His face was bruised, his neck slit, his head resting on a pillow of his own blood.

'Parker? Get up, Parker. Please, get up.'

His eyes were wide open. Only... only he didn't have eyes. Those milky, sightless orbs that saw more than they should, that magically infused the ink etched into my skin, had been torn from their sockets. Parker looked up at me with black, empty hollows, his mouth slightly ajar.

I was shivering. The room had turned cold. No, the whole world had.

'Get up, Parker,' I repeated quietly.

I was so wrapped in the cotton wool cocoon of shock that it took me a second to realise that Kirklander was lying at my feet.

I turned just in time to see the butt of a gun rushing towards my temple, then my switch flicked off.

5

B efore the black took me, I had time to think one quick, certain thought:

I'm dead.

I knew it. A tendon snapped in my brain the moment I saw what was laid out behind that shop counter. The moment I saw Parker's lifeless, maimed corpse. My body, my mind, they just gave up on me. I resigned myself to my fate at once. I was dead, and that was that.

Well, surprise, it wasn't.

Sound crept into me as I slowly regained consciousness, but the world remained dark. For a brief moment, panic threatened to overwhelm me as I pictured Parker's face—his eyeballs scooped out of his head—and wondered if the same had been done to me. If, while I slept, my eyes had been torn from their sockets and ground underfoot like discarded cigarettes. But no, as I regained my composure and the carousel of worst case scenarios flitting through my head stopped spinning, I knew that wasn't true. I wasn't blind, I'd just been blindfolded. The relief made me gasp.

Knocked out again. When were people going to get the

message? If you're going to take out Erin Banks, you'd better do it while you have the chance. Don't crack me over the skull and tie me to a chair. Don't coldcock me from behind and string me up from the rafters. If you want to put me down, do it quiet and do it quick. Because if you ever do me wrong and let me wake up, I swear on all the books that were ever printed, I will snap every bone in your body twice.

Time to assess how much shit I was in, and how exactly I was going to get out of it. I sniffed the air discreetly. The place I was being held in was damp, and had a stale, loamy smell. I was laid out on a cold floor that felt like stone, blindfolded but not gagged. Whoever it was that had taken me wanted me blind, but didn't care if I yelled or screamed or begged for help. That meant two things. One, my captors were probably looking forward to hearing me break, and two, even if I did beg for mercy, nobody in a position to help me was going to hear it. Just as well I don't do begging.

I strained my ears, but I couldn't detect another presence in the room. Was I alone? I wanted to get to my feet, but I wasn't prepared to try until I knew for sure that I wasn't being watched. Right now, I had the element of surprise, and I wasn't ready to give away the fact that I was awake. Not yet. Not until I'd gathered all the information I could on my situation.

I moved my arms, just slightly, and felt metal scrape against my wrists. I was wearing shackles, and from the weight of them, it seemed they were attached to chains, no doubt attached to the wall or the floor. Either way, the manacles felt too solid for me to break free of, even with Parker's tattoos augmenting my strength. No, I was stuck for now.

But stuck where, and by whom? Was it the pig who brought me here? Had he tailed me and Kirklander back from the Library of the Uncanny in that floating red ball of his? But then that didn't explain what had happened at Black Cat Ink, did it? Unless... maybe the pig had got ahead of us somehow, and killed Parker to send a message. A warning to stay clear of The Tenth and stop asking questions about the prophecy. Was that it? Had the Red-Eyed Man's crony murdered my friend?

A low moan caught my attention. A man? It sounded like a man. Was that Kirklander? I pictured him landing at my feet back at Black Cat Ink. Dead? My captor hadn't done me in, no reason to assume they'd treated him any differently. Another moan, same sound, a little quieter this time. The voice was close, but muffled. Behind a door?

Parker's mutilated face swam into my mind's eye, but I did my best to dismiss it. I had to. I couldn't afford to get emotional and let my feelings rise to the surface. Not now, not yet. I needed to be clear, to be sharp. If I let Parker's murder swamp me, I was done for. Make a wrong move now, bolt before the moment was right, and I'd only end up joining him.

A key scraped in a lock several metres away. I heard footsteps on flagstones. One person. One small person. The pig? No, the footfalls were too soft to be trotters.

'Stop pretending,' said the person who'd joined me, 'I can tell you're awake. Awake and very confused, I'll bet.'

It was a girl's voice, light and confident. A voice I recognised.

'Sophia Galoffi,' I said, sitting up and leaning back against a stone wall.

'Hello, again. We do keep crossing paths, don't we?'

Sophia Galoffi: Layton and Millie Galoffi's power-hungry daughter. A girl who'd murdered both of her siblings to ensure that she'd be the one to take over the family business when her parents called it a day. An empire of criminality, fear, and death that young Sophia had spilled gallons of blood to control, despite the fact she was barely in double digits.

'You know,' I said, giving my manacles a shake, 'if you want me to come over and hang out, you can just send a text.'

Sophia laughed and I wanted to break her scrawny neck.

What the hell was going on? Why had the Galoffis murdered Parker and taken me prisoner? More to the point, why now? I had a Red-Eyed Man to hunt down. I didn't have time for this side quest shit.

Sophia tugged off my blindfold to reveal her pale, narrow face. She smiled, revealing two rows of small teeth surrounded by way too much gum. Her thin, lank hair hung down in front of me like a pair of black drapes.

I wrinkled my nose. 'Damn, girl. I know a place that does a volumising shampoo that'd sort that mess right out.'

I knew where I was being kept the moment I clocked Sophia's voice. I'd been there before. The basement torture room beneath the Galoffi mansion where I'd once watched Layton beat a crazy woman to death with a claw hammer. I wondered if that was going to be my future, too.

'How's the head?' asked Sophia. 'I hear Grigor, my favourite bodyguard, gave you quite the whack.'

'It hurts like a motherfucker, thanks for asking.' I rubbed the back of my skull, but only for effect. My tattoos had already repaired the damage. 'Say, Soph, do mummy and daddy know you have a visitor?'

I peeled a glance over the steeple of the girl's pointy shoulder blade to see if I could get a look outside my cell, but all I saw was a closed door. I remembered from my previous visit that the torture basement housed several chambers. No doubt the moaning I'd heard was coming from from a neighbouring one, and I wanted to see if it belonged to the person I hoped it did.

'He's not dead,' said Sophia, catching my glance.

'Who?' I asked, as nonchalantly as I could.

'The hot man. The one you love.'

'Not ringing any bells,' I replied.

'He might die soon, though. Probably will. I was thinking of taking him apart in front of you, piece by piece,' she trilled in her sing song voice. 'Taking his fingers, his hands, his arms, his legs. What do you think of that? Would you still love him if he was just a torso and a head?'

'How about you stop playing silly bastards and tell me why I'm here?'

More to the point, why had she done away with Parker, one of the few people in the world who mattered to me? What had I done to deserve that? Okay, stupid question, I'd done enough terrible things in my time to warrant my murder several times over—not to mention the death of anyone who had the misfortune of knowing me—but specifically, what had I done to piss off the Galoffis?

Well, again, several things, but which of them did they actually know about? There was Albert Galoffi, of course, a cousin of Layton and Millie's, who I'd been hired to off, but that was years ago. Had that spot of murder finally come back to bite me on the arse?

'Look how you sit and wonder,' said Sophia.

'Not wondering, just a touch of trapped wind.'

Sophia smiled and crossed the cell to inspect a stout wooden bench, upon which were laid out all manner of sharp and pointy metal implements, each stained brown with old blood. Her fingers stroked across the torture tools with a featherlite touch.

'I liked the Solomon Twins,' she said. 'They looked funny.'

Ah. And oh. And *shit*.

The Solomons. The original gruesome twosome. A vicious set of conjoined sisters who oversaw a local drug operation, now defunct. The mother of a girl who overdosed on the drug they were manufacturing hired me to shut down the operation, and the twins, with extreme prejudice. I'd done so, happily. The thing was, though, it turned out the Solomons weren't the top of the tree. Oh, they ran the factory, all right, but they did so under the ample wing of the Galoffi family, who took a significant cut of their profits. And here's where it gets really sticky: see, the Solomons' drug had been bringing in some serious profit, so the Gallofis were none too pleased when someone burned down their factory and turned off the money spigot. Damn it. I thought I'd gotten away clean, but somehow the family joined up the dots and saw my face staring back at them.

'You're wondering how, aren't you?' asked Sophia, as if reading my mind. 'You're not half as clever as you think, you know. My parents knew all along. What did you think, that the twin you let live wouldn't tell us the truth?'

Of course. One of the sisters had survived the factory fire and come after me. I assumed she was acting independently, but she must have been acting on orders. She must have reported to Layton and been told to clean up her mess. Only she didn't, because I killed her, and I'd been twisting in the wind ever since.

'So quiet. Nothing to say?' said Sophia, looking back at me over her shoulder. 'Usually, you're so quick to talk. So keen to let fly an oh-so-funny one-liner.'

I strained against my chains, testing their strength.

Sophia turned to me fully and tugged at a leather necklace, drawing a heavy, iron key from beneath her simple, grey dress. 'Not without this, you won't,' she said. 'I made sure those chains were built to withstand a tractor pull. Sorry.' She returned to her implements. 'Now, which one shall I use on you first? I'm spoiled for choice.'

I let the chains go slack. 'So what's the play here? Torture and kill me? That what we're up to?'

'Good plan, don't you think?'

'It won't work, I can tell you that right now. Not the killing bit, anyway. Believe me, plenty have tried and just as many have failed.'

'Oh, don't worry about me, I'm good at getting what I want,' Sophia replied. 'Ask either of my brothers; you'll be meeting them soon enough.'

Oof, good line. This little bitch was the real deal.

'Aha!' she exclaimed with childish glee. 'This one.' She scooped up one of the tools and turned to me, holding it aloft. A simple, thin metal spike, its razor-sharp point chromed by the light of the cell's single, overhead bulb. 'I call this one Jimmy. Jimmy the Spike. Say hello to Jimmy.'

'Hello, Jimmy.'

Sophia grinned, showing me that gummy smile again. 'I think he likes you,' she declared, walking towards me, her eyes unblinking, her smile stretched as wide as could be.

'How about you and me make a deal?' I suggested, scurrying backwards on my arse and pressing my back against the cold, stone wall.

'No deal.'

I readied myself to lash out at her when she got too close, but before I had the chance, she pulled a nearby lever and my chains hauled me upright with a series of loud, screeching clanks, pinning my wrists to the cell wall. I strained to pull my arms free, to lunge forward and throttle the life out of my captor, but the chains held me tight. Sophia wasn't kidding when she said those things were built to last.

'Let's get to work, shall we?' said Sophia.

Without ceremony, she shoved Jimmy the Spike into the meat of my thigh and whisked it about. I let out a cry despite myself, the chains the only things keeping me from crumbing to the ground.

'Describe it,' she said.

'What?' I cried, my jeans staining dark as blood bloomed around the spike.

'The pain. Describe it. Give it a score out of ten.'

'How about you eat my arse?'

Sophia wiggled the spike in my leg some more.

I hissed through gritted teeth. 'Call it a six,' I said. 'Could do better.'

Sophia nodded and pulled the spike out of my leg. She looked at the blood as it dripped from the spike, and leaned in to give it a sniff.

'You are one sick puppy, Sophia.'

The little girl shrugged. 'Runs in the family.' She brought the spike to my face and tenderly tapped the flat of it against my cheek, the way a slaughterhouse worker might pat the rump of a heifer before they stuck the bolt gun in their head.

'Speaking of family,' I said, 'where are Layton and Millie?'

'Hm? Oh. Upstairs somewhere, watching TV. They're hooked on this show called *Drag Race*, have you seen it?' She turned and headed back to the tool desk.

My tattoos glowed red as the wound in my thigh knitted together and the pain in my leg evaporated. 'Can't say I have,' I replied.

'You should really watch it. Such delightful freaks.'

'Sure. *They're* the weird ones.'

Sophia ignored me. 'My parents are rather eager to retire now since I've proved myself more than capable of running their interests. They'll steer me for a year or two, then step away completely, leaving me to run the family business any way I see fit.'

'They must be so proud. You're like a prodigy.'

'A prodigy of pain.'

Damn. This girl was edgier than a dodecahedron.

'You know, kiddo, no one likes a smart-arse.'

'You think I'd be in this business if I cared about people *liking* me?' she replied, offering a smile of shark-like proportions.

She was one scary little kid. A scary little kid who was going to kill the shit out of me if I didn't get the upper hand soon. I needed a plan. Something. *Anything*.

My tattoos burned as I yanked at the chains, trying to uproot them from the wall.

'Ah, now what about this one next?' asked Sophia, turning to me and brandishing a tool that looked a bit like a pizza slicer, only spikier.

'Mine's a Meat Feast, ta,' I said, hoping she couldn't see the sweat prickling my brow. 'No olives.'

Sophia pressed a rotating metal circle covered in jagged teeth into my stomach, hard enough to hurt, but not quite hard enough to break the skin.

'Does this one have a name?' I asked, forcing a grin.

'I call him Slicey.'

'Adorable.'

My muscles tensed as Sophia pressed down and the teeth bit into my stomach.

'I could work for you,' I rasped, clamping down on the

pain. 'For your family. For free. As long as you like. Any job you like.'

'Not interested.' She pushed, and the slicer rotated as she cut a path across my midriff.

I had to keep talking. Had to try and shut out the pain as the disc gouged open a second layer of skin. 'Mistake... that's a mistake...'

'It is? Why?'

'If you're taking over—if you really want to run this town —you'll need to work with the best. Sharez Jek's dead. I killed him. That makes me the best.'

Sophia stopped and frowned. 'How can you be the best if you got caught? If your friend died? If you're about to die?'

I shrugged. 'We all have our off days.'

Sophia pressed hard, smiling again as I cried out. 'Better than a six?'

'Oh, a seven at least.'

She pushed on the slicer with all of her weight. I felt like my guts were getting a root canal. I clamped my eyes shut, my mind searching desperately for release, for some way to escape the torment, but the pain cancelled out any hope of rational thinking. Try as I might, I couldn't formulate a thought, the hurt was just too pervasive.

Sophia leaned back, shifting her weight to her rear heel. The world returned to me as she used her skinny fingers to peel back my eyelids. 'I wonder if I'll get a ten from you before you pass out and I have to wake you up again?'

She wasn't going for the idea of me working for her, that much was obvious. Maybe she sensed that I'd renege on my offer and murder her skinny arse the first chance I got. Or maybe—and this seemed about as likely—she just really wanted to kill me. For the sheer pleasure of it. To send a message, too. Don't fuck with the Galoffis, especially not *this* Galoffi.

Time to try another angle.

'You know, I reckon a man would have brought me to a ten ages ago,' I said.

Sophia took a pause and looked back at me with darkness in her eyes. 'Is that right?'

'Oh, yeah. Not as keen on the foreplay. You know men, always wanting to get straight to business, am I right?'

Her top lip pulled back, revealing a set of small teeth. 'What are you doing?'

'I'm just saying, I'm sure one of your brothers would have gotten to the point by now.'

'Unlikely, seeing as I murdered them.'

She placed Slicey on the workbench and began to ponder which torture tool to take up next.

'I know what it's like,' I continued, 'a woman in a man's world.'

Sophia snorted. 'A "man's world"? Do you know how silly you sound?'

'Murder is a man's business. That's what they told me when I started out as a killer for hire. They said the job asked too much of a woman. Ate away at us more than it did men, because we have more empathy.'

'Not all of us.' Sophia lifted a spiked mallet, shook her head, and placed it back down.

While her back was turned I strained at my chains again. I didn't need to break them, I just needed a little give, that was all. Maybe I couldn't snap the chains, but I might be able to force the mechanism that pulled me back.

'Women have to work twice as hard in this world,' I said. 'I had to murder so many people before the real pay days started rolling my way. Kirklander? He was earning top dollar a few kills in. Talk about unfair. Talk about inequality.'

Sophia didn't respond, but I could read her body language, she was listening, taking it all in.

'Then there's you. Little Sophia Galoffi. Even after offing your eldest brother, you were still gonna get overlooked. Why? Because you don't have a cock, that's why. Where's the justice in that?'

Sophia turned back to me with a bone saw in her hand. I strained against the mechanism, trying not to make it too obvious what I was doing. Distracting her by talking, by pushing her buttons.

'It's a moot point,' she replied. 'I got what I deserved in the end. I made it happen.'

'Yeah, but do you reckon anyone respects you for it? I'm talking about the respect one of your brothers would have gotten just for existing. I seriously doubt it. Fuck the patriarchy, right?'

'They will respect me,' she snarled, and slashed at my arm with the saw.

I cried out, blood dripping from the ragged gash, but I kept on. Kept on talking, kept on straining against the mechanism. I just needed to make the cogs skip back a tooth or two, that's all. Give me a little slack when I needed it. I could do it. I could. I had to, because if I didn't, I'd never see outside of that basement again.

'I'm just as good as any boy,' said Sophia. 'Better. Twice as good. I killed them. Killed my so-called superiors, just like I killed your boss.'

Parker.

She slashed at me again, opening a deep would across my chest.

'Is that a nine?'

'Not even close,' I replied, lying through my teeth.

'He tried. Tried to stop us as we broke into his grotty little establishment, but we knew what we were dealing with, and we took him down. The noises he made as I removed his useless eyes... as I dug my fingers into the sockets and plucked them out, one by one. You should have heard him.'

I couldn't let her distract me. Couldn't let my anger rise and knock me off track. I was getting there. This was working. My muscles ached as I pulled and pulled. Was that a little give? I needed more. More than that. I needed her close.

'I bet your dad's gutted you're taking over,' I said. 'I mean, come on, he even chose a baby over you.'

'Shut up,' she squealed, slashing again and again, turning my body into a bloody game of noughts and crosses.

I ignored it. Pain was nothing. Pain was temporary. Just push on, Erin. Push on.

'The shame he must feel, forced to hand the family business over to his little girl. Jesus, he must feel like a right laughing stock.'

'I said, shut up.'

'You're a fucking baby, Soph. A little girl walking around in her daddy's big shoes, trying to play the grown-up.'

'Enough!' She strode over to the desk, threw down the bone saw, and grabbed for a meat cleaver. 'I'm bored of you now.'

She stomped towards me, anger clouding her senses. This was it, my one chance. It had to happen now.

I screamed, my tattoos flooding with magic, and I pushed forward, body straining against the chains—

And then there it was. As Sophia buried the meat cleaver in my stomach, I heard the mechanism screech, felt the chains loosen, and yelled out in triumph. The metal in my guts barely registered as I reached out my hands and found Sophia's neck.

'No,' she whimpered.

'This is for Parker.'

I craned forward and sunk my teeth into her throat, tearing out her carotid artery. Her blood hosed my face, turning it slick and red. Sophia cried like the child she was, her legs kicking, body trembling.

And then the little bitch died.

6

I didn't let Sophia's lifeless body fall to the floor. I needed it. But first, I had to catch my breath. Oh, and get the fucking meat cleaver out of my guts.

Jaw set, body trembling, I gripped the handle. 'Okay. Just like a Band Aid. Nice and quick...'

I breathed in once then yanked the blade out of me, adding another geyser of blood to the cell wall. I screamed out good and loud. Now my torturer was dead, I didn't mind giving voice to the pain. Besides, it's not like I was going to draw any unwanted attention my way – what did someone passing the door of a torture basement expect to hear besides a prisoner's anguished cries?

Hand shaking, I reached for the leather strap around Sophia's neck and pulled it sharply so it snapped. I pushed Sophia's corpse away from me, the key to the manacles slithering from beneath the neckline of her dress as she fell away. I slid the key into my metal bonds and twisted, popping the manacles. I was free. I slid down the wall, putting a hand to the gaping wound in my stomach, and tried to slow my breathing.

It was okay.

Everything was okay.

I'd survived.

My life support was plugged in now. I just had to wait this out, let my tattoos get to work, let them heal me. I could only hope nobody came to check on Sophia's progress before I was back in fighting shape again.

As I sat there, crumpled, my wounds slowly starting to fuse together, I thought about Parker. I wondered what he'd been thinking when the insane little girl and her henchman forced their way into his parlour and murdered him. I wondered, in his final moments, if he blamed me.

I couldn't afford to think like that. Parker knew what kind of a business we were in. We swam with sharks. Chances were, none of us was going to live long enough to enjoy our retirement. Sooner or later, a Sophia would show her fin, then her teeth.

No, all Parker would have been thinking was, '*You better get me some revenge, girl.*'

I smiled, sadly. 'I did, Parks. I did.'

I looked down when I realised the pain in my stomach had subsided. The final cleaver wound had vanished. I was healed.

I grabbed the cleaver and stuck it in Sophia's head. No idea why, but it made me feel good.

Okay, time to get going.

A moan, same as earlier.

'Kirklander?'

I exited the cell and emerged into a short corridor lined with a row of iron-banded doors either side. I peered through the peepholes in each door as I passed them, searching for the source of the sound. I found each little room empty until I reached the last one. Inside, curled up on the floor and still unconscious, was Kirklander.

'Oi, wake up,' I hissed.

'Five more minutes,' he slurred, and rolled over.

I froze as footsteps echoed past the door leading up to the ground floor. I should just leave. Save my own skin. He'd left me to rot in a prison cell before, why shouldn't I return the favour?

I looked back through the peephole and knew I was fooling myself. I wasn't going to leave Kirlander behind, and something told me, if our situation was reversed, he wouldn't leave me either. Not any more.

I pressed my mouth right up to the peephole. 'Wake up,' I barked, rattling the cell door.

He sat upright like I'd jabbed his heart with a syringe full of adrenaline. 'What? Huh? Where...?' He looked around wildly before his eyes settled on me. 'Weren't we just at Parker's? Oh... Parker...'

I pressed my forehead up against his cell door. 'Yeah. Dead. I was just tortured by his killer, Sophia Galoffi.'

'Shit.'

'Don't worry, I murdered the little cow.'

'That's my girl.'

I smiled. 'Come on, we have to get you out of there before the elder Galoffis come calling.'

I backed up a couple of steps, ready to fire up my tats and kick down the door.

'Great idea, let's scoot,' said Kirklander, clambering to his feet. 'Thanks, uh, for not, you know, legging it.'

'You'd have done the same.'

His eyes met mine through the peephole and didn't waver. 'Yeah, I would.'

It was a nice moment, somewhat spoiled by the fact that

Layton and Millie Galoffi chose that exact second to descend the stairs into the basement. They were there to check in on their bloodthirsty child, Layton with his raffish waxed moustache, and Millie immaculately turned out as always, her flawless, porcelain white skin luminous against her tall, black beehive.

Two things happened then.

First, the Galoffis saw me, unshackled and unharmed.

Then they saw their daughter's body in the open cell at the end of the corridor, a meat cleaver buried in her skull.

Millie's scream rang out.

I turned to Kirklander's peephole. 'Should have just left you behind,' I sighed.

'Yup,' he agreed. 'Take a note for next time.'

'What have you done?' Layton demanded, his face twisted into a gargoyle's grimace.

'Yeah, sorry about that,' I said, thumbing over my shoulder, 'made a bit of a mess in there. Feel free to hang on to my security deposit.'

'My daughter. My successor. I'm going to kill you.'

The time for witty repartee was over. I knew how dangerous Layton and Millie could be. They weren't human, after all, just monsters in people suits. I needed to get on the front foot fast, or I'd be seeing Sophia again much sooner than I liked.

I sucked in a breath and magic soaked into my tattoos, firing up my synapses and juicing my muscles. Growling like a lioness, I launched a fist at Layton's neck, but he caught it and twisted, plucking me from the ground and sending me flying down the short corridor and back into my old holding cell. The table of torture tools broke in two as I crashed down, the metal implements clattering and scattering across the stone floor.

Shit. Apparently, Layton was in possession of some next level kung-fu style skills. Who knew?

Millie loped into the cell and dropped to her knees, cradling Sophia's corpse with her one good arm. Her weeping eyes locked on to mine. 'You're going to die for this.'

'Ladies first.' I grabbed a vicious-looking knife from the scattered torture tools and tossed it at her with a flick of the wrist, embedding it in her sternum.

The result was not as expected. She should have fallen back, should have choked and died, but instead, Millie Galoffi plucked the blade from her chest and laughed.

'You think you can kill my sister with a knife?' said Layton, approaching his wife, a mad gleam in his eyes.

Yeah, don't forget, the Galoffis might be married, might have had three kids together, but they were also brother and sister. That's a ten out of ten on the *Yikes*-ometer.

Millie stood, brandishing the oddly bloodless knife. 'We cannot be killed.'

'But we *can* kill,' said Layton.

Ah, yeah, that little factoid had slipped my mind in the rush to keep hold of my own life. I'd heard a rumour that the elder Galoffis were difficult to put down. No, more than difficult – word was it was entirely impossible to separate them from their "alive" status. That their souls were hidden somewhere safe and sound, and as long as they remained that way, the Galoffis couldn't be killed. Which kinda put me in a shitty spot.

'Shame you didn't do some of that soul shit with your kids,' I said, taking a step back. 'Three born, three dead. I'd stay well away from Mumsnet if I were you, they can get a bit judgy about that sort of stuff.'

Millie screamed and lashed out with the knife, slashing through the fabric of my vest as I hopped away just in time.

For all the good it would do me. I was backed up against the cell wall now, the incestuous, impossible-to-kill Galoffis stalking towards me with lethal intent.

So it was a good job Kirklander decided not to save his own skin, slipped out of his cell, and joined the fight.

A wave of purple fire blasted through the cell door, lifting a shocked Layton and Millie off their feet and smashing them against the stone wall I'd only recently been manacled to. I winced as I heard bones break on contact.

'What the f...?'

'Looked as if you could use a hand,' said Kirklander, swaggering in and blowing some purple magic off his finger like it was gunsmoke.

'I was on top of things.'

'Maybe later, if you're good,' he replied with a wolfish grin, and god dammit if a box of butterflies didn't open up in my stomach.

I had no intention of sticking around to find out how badly Kirklander's flashy new magic had damaged the Galoffis. Instead, I grabbed Kirk's elbow and steered him towards the exit. 'Come on, we've gotta go.'

'Man, you are hot to trot!'

I gave him a dig in the shoulder and shoved him through the cell door, into the corridor beyond, hustling him in the direction of the staircase that led out of the basement.

'Going somewhere?' asked Layton, up on his feet again.

He'd snatched up Jimmy the Spike while Kirk and I were busy flirting. The Galoffi patriarch tossed the weapon with deadly accuracy, or at least it would have been deadly if Kirk hadn't raised a hand, his splayed fingers sparking with purple static, and halted Jimmy mid-air.

'What the hell, Kirk?' I gasped, impressed but surprised by the sudden emergence of his boss-level magical skills.

'I know, I'm even turning myself on.'

Layton grabbed the bone saw off the ground and sprinted forward, white-lipped with rage. I tore the door of Kirk's cell from its hinges and launched it in Layton's direction. The lump of wood struck him hard in the face, halting his progress and sent him crashing to the floor.

I made a pained whistle. 'Indestructible or not, that had to hurt.'

Millie stepped forward, her face dented but not bloody, her beehive slightly askew. 'You will not leave our home alive,' she growled.

Kirklander had other ideas. He clicked his fingers, and Jimmy the Spike turned so his business end was pointing Millie's way. Another click, and the shaft of tapered metal hurtled towards her, striking her in the neck and pinning her to the wall.

'Stick around,' said Kirklander.

'Really?' I replied, rolling my eyes back so far it's a wonder I didn't catch sight of my own brain.

Layton rose from the ground and used his hands to right what had, only moments ago, been a shattered neck. Meanwhile, Millie pulled the spike from her neck and tossed it aside.

'Maybe we should get the fuck out of here,' I suggested, as the hole in her neck sealed shut.

These two were made of tough stuff. Even with my enhanced powers of recuperation, I was pretty sure a hole in the throat or a broken neck would be the end of me.

We ran for the exit, racing up the spiral stairs, Layton and Millie snapping at our heels, howling like rabid animals. At the top of the steps was a stout wooden door, which I slammed shut behind us and turned the lock on. It wouldn't hold them for long.

'Step back,' said Kirklander, before clapping his hands and showing me some more of the old razzle dazzle.

A magical barrier shimmered to life in front of the basement door, glowing like liquid gold.

'No staff for that, either?'

'Nope,' he replied casually. 'Should keep them stuck in there long enough for us to escape.'

I opened my mouth to respond, only to go flying backwards like someone had tugged my ripcord. The gout of blood that erupted from my shoulder and spattered Kirklander's chest told me that I'd just been shot.

'Motherfucker,' I said, picking myself up and seeing five Galoffi goons pouring down the hallway at us, pistols in hand.

My tattoos flared as I clenched my fists and I ran towards the suited monkeys.

'Other way!' yelled Kirklander, but the red mist was upon me.

I barely even felt the next two bullets that tore through my thigh and arm as I charged forward. My fists met jaws, met necks, met ribs, my knees and boots turned testicles into mincemeat. I felt good, fluid, strong, unstoppable. I was Keanu Reeves in *The Matrix*, or a more recent yet appropriate reference for you young 'uns. I don't know, grab one that works for you.

Within ten seconds, the fight was over and the dead bodies of the goons laid scattered around me like toppled statues.

'That,' said Kirklander, 'was hot.'

I grinned as my bullet wounds closed up, but the fight wasn't over yet. The basement door shook and splintered as Millie and Layton fought to break free.

'Okay,' I said, '*now* let's scoot.'

We ran for the front door, both grinning like fools, shooting through the exit and into the grounds outside.

'This should buy us a little time,' said Kirklander, clapping his hands together again.

Another magical barrier appeared, a circle, large enough to wrap around the entire Galoffi mansion. 'Now let's put some distance between us and this fucked up Addams Family.'

'No,' I said.

'Uh, come again?'

I thought about Parker, lying on his parlour floor. He was dead because of the Galoffis. Not just Sophia, but the whole clan. I glanced over to one of the many expensive cars parked in front of the mansion.

'Can you open up a gap in that circle of yours?'

Kirklander shrugged. 'Easy.'

'Then do it.'

I ran for the nearest car, a black stretch limo, the same one Layton and Millie's goons had used to cart me away after they beat the shit out of me on the seafront a few months back. I wrenched open the car's locked door before slotting in behind the steering wheel. No key on offer, but that didn't matter. I dug my fingers into the ignition and pulled it free, grabbing the loose wires and twisting them together. The car started.

I looked out towards Kirk, who gave me a thumbs up.

'Big gap right in front of you,' he yelled.

I stomped on the accelerator. The back wheels kicked up some gravel, then the limo went hurtling towards the mansion. I was playing chicken with a house, and the house was going to lose.

The car crashed through the large wooden entrance doors and into the Galoffi gothic mansion before coming to a squealing stop in front of the foyer's grand, sweeping staircase.

Ignoring the mild whiplash, I hopped out of the limo and twisted open the cap to the fuel tank. Tearing a piece of material from my top, I stuffed it inside the hole, pulled out a lighter, and touched a flame to it, turning the car into a giant Molotov cocktail. I watched for a second as the flame took hold, then began to back away.

'Fuck you, you flotilla of turds!' I called out, then ran from the mansion and stopped by Kirklander's side. 'Close the circle.'

'Your wish is my command,' he said, and clicked his fingers, the gap in the circle of protection shimmering briefly as it sealed shut.

Kirklander and I linked arms as we watched the limo explode, the ensuing carnage contained by his magical ward. Angry flames groped against the inside of the impenetrable bubble like a pervert's hands, claiming everything within.

'How long will that thing hold?' I asked.

'These days, at least an hour.'

Good. Long enough for the fire to rage through every nook and cranny of that place. Long enough for it to find Layton and Millie Galoffi, and the corpse of their evil daughter, and turn them all to ash.

We stayed right to the end, not leaving until the Galoffi empire had fully burned to the ground.

7

The Galoffi home was situated just outside Brighton, so rather than taking a long walk back to the city, I hotwired another of their cars, a vintage Rolls-Royce Phantom, and drove us back in style.

'You're sure?' asked Kirklander as I stared out of the window of the Rolls towards the entrance of Black Cat Ink.

Parker was still in there, his body at least. I wasn't just going to leave him like that for someone else to deal with. He was my boss. My friend. The guy who gave me the keys to the Uncanny Kingdom. Without him, I had no idea where I'd be at this point, but if I had to hazard a guess, I'd go with dead.

I got out of the car and walked towards the tattoo parlour, the ground beneath me feeling like melted tar, my every footstep dragging. I pushed open the door and ground to a stop. I turned, looking back over my shoulder to the spot Parker and I had first met, a low wall on the opposite side of the road.

'You ever gonna come in, girl?'

The first words he'd ever spoken to me. I thought I'd

been so slick, so sly, scoping out his parlour for the best part of a week, watching his clientele come and go. Scribbling notes in my little pad about vampires and trolls, all the while thinking no one was any the wiser, that I was invisible. It was six days before Parker finally gave in and came out to ask me what I wanted. He was blind of course, but somehow he'd sensed me keeping an eye on the place, working up the courage to go in and look for answers. He'd opened the door for me that day, and now here I was, opening a door that led to his dead body.

I stepped into Black Cat Ink, slowly trudging down the short set of steps to the parlour, Kirklander following behind. It was the middle of the night, creeping up on three in the morning, and the shop was deathly quiet. Parker had been killed after business hours, and had remained here, undiscovered, as the night crept on. But now I'd come back for him to make sure that his remains were properly taken care of.

I could see his feet, still sticking out from behind the counter.

'What are we gonna do?' asked Kirklander.

What *was* I going to do? Parker had no family, no next of kin. What happened now was up to me.

I nodded as I arrived at a decision. 'We're gonna bury him. Lay him to rest.'

Kirklander sighed as he crouched next to Parker's body. 'We crossed paths a lot over the years, me and him. Put a lot of business my way. I know he didn't like me all that much...'

'Understandable.'

'...But I always respected the guy. He got me gigs when I could barely find my arse with both hands.' He patted Parker's leg then stood, walking away to give me some time.

I took his place, crouching down, trying not to look at the empty hollows where Parker's eyes used to be.

'I owe everything to him,' I said, my fingers stroking the exposed tattoos across my collarbone. 'Without him, I'd have no magic. No power. No chance. I wouldn't be one step closer to figuring out what happened to James.'

'You'd never have met me, either,' Kirk added.

'Okay, so he wasn't an entirely positive influence on my life.'

'You know, words can hurt, Erin,' Kirklander replied with a grin, his green eyes twinkling.

'Hey, Parks,' I said, my hand wavering before I allowed it to rest on his boot. I didn't want to touch his skin. 'Thanks. Thanks for everything.'

'Please, you're making a ghost blush over here.'

'Sweet Jesus!' cried Kirklander, as he whirled around to find Parker stood behind him. Well, Parker's spirit at any rate, his ghost.

'Death looks good on you,' I said, standing, trying to pull the tears back into my body before they went flooding down my cheeks.

'Everything looks good on me, girl,' he replied with a grin, his teeth big and white.

'Sorry about...' I gestured towards his mostly hidden corpse.

'Chu. How'd you think I saw myself checking out? Withering away in a retirement home? Death coming for everyone in this room sooner than we'd like. That's the deal. Why we live hard and fast to pack as much as we can in, 'cos we know we on a sprint, not a marathon.'

'Hey, you didn't overhear me saying anything nice about you, right?' asked Kirklander.

'About how you respected me?'

'Yeah.'

'Not a word of it.'

'Oh, thank God.'

'Now get the hell out of here while me and my best girl say our goodbyes, you backstabbing streak of piss.'

'Will do,' said Kirklander, jogging up the stairs and out.

'Alone at last,' said Parker. 'So, you and him a thing again or what?'

'I... it's complicated.'

'It's stupid. So is he.'

'He's not stupid. Okay, he can be stupid, but he's not *stupid*.'

'You make no sense, girl.'

I smiled and sat down on the couch. Parker looked much the same as he had when he was alive, but a little insubstantial, and with his colours muted.

'What's it feel like?' I asked.

'Being dead? It don't feel like much of anything. I mean that literally. No taste, no smell, like everything got dialled down to zero.'

'Doesn't sound great.'

'Better than nothing, I guess.'

He walked over to the counter and looked down at his body.

'Pulling the eyes out of a blind man. Weird move,' he said. 'Oh! That's something good about being dead, my eyes actually work same as yours now.'

I looked up at him and realised for the first time that his eyes were no longer milky white.

'Hey! That's... well... good?'

'I gotta say, I knew you were a looker, but now I really see what that no-good dog Kirklander sees in you.'

'Are you flirting with me? Are you dead and flirting with me?'

Parker laughed and took a seat next to me. 'So. What now for you?'

'Same old same old, I guess. Murder, mayhem, money.'

'Without your ink?'

I looked down at the tattooed runes creeping out past the cuffs of my jacket. How much longer would they last? Pretty soon they'd be drained, and then what?

'Maybe now's the time,' said Parker.

'Time for what?'

'Call it quits. Walk away before you end up a dead body for someone you love to stumble across.'

I pictured Lana letting herself into my flat after a day of me not replying to her messages. Imagined her face as she found me stuck to the carpet with my own dried blood.

'I'm getting close, Parks. Really, really close to finally finding out what happened to James.'

'Answers won't do you no good if you're dead. Get out. Live a real life. Be happy.'

Our eyes met and his forehead crinkled.

'I know you've just died so this might be a little out of line, but you can fuck right off with that kind of talk.'

Parker laughed, mouth wide, head back, his crop of dreads dancing like stalks of wheat in a hurricane. 'Hey, I had to try.'

'I know. Thanks,' I said with a smile.

'I'm gonna miss you, girl.'

He shimmered, his body becoming increasingly indistinct, then it was as if he had never been there at all.

'Bye, Parker.'

8

There's a place on the outskirts of Brighton. Well, the outskirts and underneath. A burial place for Uncanny types that can only be accessed through an ancient sewer grate.

Unseen under a starless night, Kirklander and I wrapped Parker's body in a torn-up length of carpet and hefted it to the Rolls I'd liberated from the Galoffis, placing him in the boot before we headed west in the direction of the Resting Place.

I could smell Layton Galoffi's cigar smoke inside the car, infecting the leather upholstery. I wondered if he and his sister/wife were actually dead. Had they exaggerated their ability to cling to life no matter what? A self-published myth to deter any would-be competitors? Or was even being reduced to ash not beyond their powers of recuperation? Would they, even now, be gathering together, flake by flake, ready to come after me anew?

But that was a worry for another day. Right then and there, I had bigger and more immediate fish to fry.

Twenty minutes later, Kirklander wrenched open a rusty

grate and clambered down a ladder until he was underground. I lowered Parker, still wrapped in carpet, down to him, and between us we carried his body deep into the earth. Illuminated by a globe of iridescent light that Kirklander conjured, we followed the tunnels in silence for three miles until they opened out into a vast cavern covered in a mile-deep blanket of soil.

The Resting Place.

A graveyard for the Uncanny.

There were no stone gravestones or gothic mausoleums; each body was marked with a simple, fist-sized, glistening black rock.

'A lot of crazy-strange-magical dead things hidden in here,' said Kirklander.

'Shut up, Kirk.'

'Copy that.'

A shovel leant against the wall by the entrance. I grabbed it and we carried Parker out into the cavern until we found a likely spot. Then we dug. When the hole was big enough, we placed Parker gently into the earth and covered him, placing a rock on top.

I didn't say any words. I'd already said what I wanted to say. We walked back in silence. By the time we were sat in the Rolls again, picking soil from under our fingernails, the morning sun had risen.

'You okay?' asked Kirklander.

'Never better.'

Parker was dead, and the honest truth was, I'd spent most of the last few hours thinking about myself. Worrying what my future meant without him. I was on borrowed time, that much was obvious. My tattoos wouldn't last much longer, they'd weaken and finally be rejected, and then what?

I'd be powerless.

Just me. Just my given body, my given strength, my given weaknesses. Could I really carry on without Parker's ink? I had to. I didn't have a choice, especially now I was so close. I had to find The Tenth. Had to find the Red-Eyed Man. Tattoos or no tattoos, I had to keep following the thread, no matter where it led, until I found out the truth about my brother.

I twisted the exposed ignition wires together again, and the engine roared to life. As we drove, something bad happened. Maybe not as bad as being tortured by a psycho-pre-teen, or finding your friend's eyeless corpse, but still pretty bad. Kirklander and I started talking about... *our feelings*.

'So, are we gonna get into what happened the other week or not?' he asked.

'No idea what you're talking about,' I replied, fully, painfully, awfully aware of what he was talking about.

'Babe, you came to my place and said those three words.'

'Your breath stinks?'

Kirklander laughed, then slyly cupped a hand to his mouth and checked to see if I was telling the truth.

'Look, I know what I said,' I told him.

'That you love me.'

My insides squeezed so tight I almost threw up. 'Yeah. That... what you just said.'

'So... do you?'

'Well...' I made a lot of strange, dismissive noises as I struggled to figure out what to say next. 'I was out of my mind, okay? You know that.'

'Right. Thought so.'

'Good. I was being pushed to the brink of suicide by a

crazy half-demon, I'd have said anything to find a safe space. I just needed something to cling on to, that's all.'

Kirklander frowned and nodded. 'So you don't love me?'

'Uh, no. Course not. Obviously.' We drove in silence for a couple of minutes. I'd say it was a little uncomfortable, but that would be doing those two, excruciating minutes a grave disservice. 'How can either of us really love anyone? I mean, do you know what that even is?'

'I've heard a lot of songs about it, but no.'

'Exactly. We're killers. Bad people. Deep as a puddle. Me and you don't love.'

'Right. Although...'

'What?'

'You don't think we can grow? Even a little?'

'You grow more than a little, am I right?' I raised a hand, ready to receive a high five. A solid dick compliment would surely divert us from this awful conversation, wouldn't it?

Kirklander left me hanging. I sighed and returned my hand to the wheel.

Okay, time to change the subject properly. 'You know, I seem to remember you wanting to tell me something important when I said those... insane words that we don't need to bring up ever again.'

'That you love me?'

'I swear to God I will make mashed potatoes out of your bollocks. What is it you were trying to tell me?'

Kirklander shrugged. 'Nothing. It was nothing.'

'It didn't seem like nothing.'

'Hey, if you can swerve the, "I love you" thing, then I can swerve the thing I don't want to bring up again, okay?'

'Even though it was nothing?'

'Exactly. I'm swerving the nothing. So it should be really easy to swerve, because there's nothing to swerve.'

'Swerve away.'

'Swerve executed.'

I double-checked how far we were from my flat. It was way too far.

'I'm gonna say something now, and I want you to be as un-smug about it as it's possible for you to be.'

'I'll try my best,' he replied, 'no promises.'

'I... need your help.'

'Well, I'm really confused as to what I've been doing so far.'

'Sarcasm is the ugly cousin of smugness.'

Kirklander let forth a long exhale. 'I already know you need my help. You don't need to ask. Your tattoos are gonna putter out soon, and if you're wanting to carry on after this red-eyed bloke, you need me.'

I swallowed down the distaste. 'Yes. Thing is, you're a twat.'

'You've brought that up before.'

'And I don't know if I can trust you.'

Kirklander shifted uncomfortably.

'Will you stand by me, with no promise of any kind of reward? Will you just help me because... it's me?' I kept my eyes on the road. I didn't think my heart could take looking at him.

'Of course,' he replied. 'From now on, the answer is always "of course".'

I nodded. I was happy with his reply, but that didn't squash down all the mistrust. 'Thing is, my entire life is built on bad decisions. Bad decisions and bad memories, and I don't want this to be another one.'

'Hey, yours is built on bad memories, mine is built on mistakes. Mistakes and regrets.'

'And selfishness. Don't forget selfishness.'

'Oh, a shit-load of selfishness.'

'Can I add stupidity to the list?'

'Only if I can add terminally sexy.'

'I'll allow it.'

Kirklander sketched out a smile. 'You want to know the stupidest thing?'

'What?'

'Hurting you. Every time I did it. Every time.'

I frowned. I nodded. I burst out laughing.

'Oh, nice, I try to be a little sincere...'

'No, no, I'm sorry, it's just...' Laughter swamped me again, filling my eyes with tears. I actually had to pull over before I crashed us both into a tree.

'I'm sorry... so sorry... you just sound... really ridiculous!'

I was bent over now, laughing so hard that no sound was coming out. Kirklander chuckled. The chuckle built, and built, until he too was roaring with laughter, sending the car rocking like the two of us were deep in the bone zone.

'Jesus,' I said, gasping for breath and wiping my eyes clear with my sleeve. 'Jesus fucking Christ, I needed that.'

I composed myself and got the car moving again. Call me stupid, plenty had before—Parker especially—but this time... God help me, this time, I believed with everything in me that Kirklander had my back. No matter what, he'd be at my side.

If this comes back to bite me on the arse, you have my signed permission to shove me off the nearest cliff.

9

With all of those unseemly sharings and icky emotional outpourings out of the way, I dropped Kirklander off at my place and told him to get a few hours sleep. Of course, he tried to convince me to do rude things with him, but I didn't have time to dick around (poor choice of words, but you know what I'm getting at).

I dumped the Galoffi car a few streets over, then collected my Porsche. When I returned later to pick up Kirklander, there would be no more breaks. No time to rest, to make house calls, to do anything other than work the case. The most important case of my life. Solving the mystery of my brother's disappearance. I was entering the endgame with my tattoos almost on empty. I knew the chances of me walking away from this one were slim. Which meant one thing. Before Kirklander and I went headfirst into this, I needed to see the woman I loved more than anything. I had to tell her what she meant to me, and I had to say goodbye.

I parked outside Lana's house and spent a minute or two psyching myself up. This wasn't going to be pretty. It was going to be ugly. It was going to be painful. I was going to see things in Lana's eyes that were going to break my heart. The selfish bit of me was screaming: *Just drive away, you idiot, you don't have time for this touchy feely shit.*

Besides, how was today different from any other day for me? Every time I stepped outside and went to work there was a fair chance of me winding up cut into chunks and thrown down the sewer to be eaten by rats.

But...

But it *was* different.

It definitely *felt* different. Like an end was fast approaching. An end to the path I'd been travelling on since the day James was taken. And maybe—probably, with my tattoos fading and Parker dead in the ground—an end to my life in general.

Yeah. I had to face her. I had to say goodbye, just in case.

I looked at myself in the rearview mirror. 'Shit. Shit-shit-bollocks-fuck-shit.'

With that motivational speech out of the way, I stepped out of the car, strode towards my cousin's house, and rang the doorbell.

'Hey,' said Lana, answering the door in scruffy dungarees, her blonde hair in disarray. An uncertain smile crossed her face. 'Was I expecting you?'

I shook my head. 'I need to... talk.'

Lana's smile faltered, and I followed her inside.

Two minutes later I was sat at her kitchen table, warming my hands around a mug of freshly-brewed coffee. I topped off my cup of lightning with a jigger of whisky from my hip flask.

'You okay there?' asked Lana.

'Yeah, just got a banger of a headache that needs fixing.'

'You know,' she replied, peering at me over the rim of

her #1 *Mum* mug, 'maybe if you stopped drinking so much you'd feel better.'

'Yeah. I'd feel pain better, I'd feel self-doubt better, I'd feel a crushing sense of dread better. Shall I go on?'

Lana frowned, then rattled her head like her brain was an Etch-a-Sketch and my bad attitude was a doodle she needed to erase. 'Sorry I look a mess,' she said. 'I just got back from the school run and it was a real war zone out there.'

I laughed. A war zone. There I was, fighting supernatural creatures and getting tortured by inhuman gangsters, but Lana was the real hero. Sure, my life was on the line and I was about to go toe-to-toe with a creature powerful enough to wipe the memory of Carlisle, an immensely powerful magician, but how could that possibly compare to offloading a couple of sprogs from the Volvo before the school bell rang?

I caught myself mid-thought. Stop being so judgmental, I told myself. Just because Lana didn't mix with the dark and dragging horrors of the Uncanny underworld, didn't mean her life was inconsequential. Lana White wasn't just some housewife marking time on her way to the grave, she was special. My cousin was the lighthouse that steered me through the choppy waters of this world. The beacon that guided me to shore when I was at my most wayward. My most lost.

She plonked herself opposite me and set her elbows on the table, fists propping her chin. 'How worried should I be?'

'Out of ten?'

'If you like.'

'Let's say a good nine and a half.'

'Shit.'

'Yeah. Big shit.'

I blew on the hot coffee and took a sip. 'Parker's dead.'

Lana's eyes snapped wide, the colour draining from her cheeks. 'What?'

'Someone found out about a job he put me on. Decided to kill him because of it. Tried to kill me, too.'

Lana came around the table and reached down to hug me. I let her.

'God, I'm so sorry. Are you okay?'

I untangled myself. 'I'm fine. Don't worry, I dealt with the people who did it.'

Lana scraped her fingers through her hair and exhaled slowly, lowering herself down on the chair next to me.

'I'm so sorry, Erin. I know what he meant to you.'

'He was my boss.'

'He was more than that.'

I lowered my eyes, focusing on the swirling grain of the tabletop.

'Wait,' said Lana, putting two and two together, 'your tattoos. What does that mean for you?'

I sighed. 'Well, it sort of leaves me up shit creek.'

'Can anyone else do them for you?'

'I don't know. Parker said his gift was rare.'

I shifted, uncomfortable. In the past I'd looked for others like Parker, just in case. I wasn't trying to leave him in the lurch, but it was a dangerous world. I always knew there was a chance something like this might happen. I hadn't looked hard enough, though, and now here I was, living on borrowed time.

'So what happens when the magic wears off?' asked Lana.

'It means that's that. Bye bye, powers. Bye bye, healing.'

Lana brightened up. She tried to play it cool, but I could

see it. It was like a flower spreading its petals. 'So... does that mean you'll stop?'

I snorted by way of reply.

'Erin, if you don't have your tattoos, you don't have a choice. You have to stop. It's too dangerous with them, but without them? I mean, how long would you feasibly last?'

'I can't stop.'

'Of course you can!'

I closed my eyes for a moment, not wanting to see the tears in Lana's. 'Magic or not, I'm part of that world. I couldn't live a normal life now even if I wanted to. Which I don't. Do you really see me getting a regular job, a nice husband, cuddling up on the couch watching Netflix on a Friday night?'

Lana swiped at her tears with the sleeve of her jumper. 'So, what? You're just going to march on towards the chopping block, is that it?'

I'd normally get angry at this point. At Lana needling me, pushing me to give up the life I'd built and return to the safety of the kind she had. But not this time. Because this time she was dead right, and I was going to ignore her anyway.

'I have to.'

'You don't, you know you don't.'

'It's James, Lana. I'm so close to finding out the truth. Honestly. I'm almost all there, I just need to hang in a little while longer.'

Her expression hardened. 'What if hanging in there kills you?'

'I've got help. Kirklander.'

She snorted derisively. 'The man who left you behind so the police could stick you in a jail cell? Well, why should I worry then?'

I slammed my mug down on the table. 'Kirk's a good guy.'

'Oh yeah, he's a real prince.'

Her furious eyes locked on mine, and then, as one, we crumbled into laughter. Two cousins, laughing in the face of death. Treating my reality with all the absurdity it deserved.

'Well, he's all I've got,' I said, getting my laughter under control.

'He's not. You've got me.'

I smiled. 'I know. But not for this. Never for this.'

Lana sagged back, defeated. She knew I was walking out of there and heading into the lion's den, and nothing she did or said was going to fix that. No begging, no cross words, no amount of love was ever going to change my mind.

'How sure are you? About James?'

'Very. I'm almost there, Lana. I need to know. And if there's any chance, any chance at all, that he's still alive, I'm going to help him.'

'And if he isn't?'

'Then I'll settle for revenge.'

'Even if it kills you?'

'I'm not scared of dying.'

'Then you're stupid.'

'Yeah, I suppose so.'

Lana stood and hugged me again. I wrapped my arms around her and held on tight. 'Don't die.'

'Promise.'

She cupped my face in her hands, her cheeks wet. 'I hate you so much.'

'Love you too,' I replied.

10

I felt drained as I headed home. First Parker's death, then his untimely burial, followed by my more-or-less "goodbye" talk with Lana. The past 24 hours had left me feeling flattened. My nerves were on edge, and my brain weighed heavy in my skull. I needed to rest. To hole up for a day or two before I got back to the business of throwing myself in harm's way.

But I didn't have time.

It felt like the dark was snapping at my heels and I had to keep moving, had to keep one step ahead of it, or it would swamp me before I got my face-to-face with the Red-Eyed Man. Before I found out the truth and did something horrible about it.

I clawed around in the glovebox of the Porsche and found a plastic tube with a couple of pills rattling around in the bottom. Uppers. They'd keep me going. Make me sharp again. Sharp as the blade I intended to slide between old Red-Eye's ribs.

I swallowed them down dry and stomped on the accelerator.

Kirklander wasn't in bed when I got home, he was slumped on the couch in my pigsty of a lounge watching daytime TV.

'Did you know your cooker doesn't work?' he asked, looking up and scratching his belly.

'Yeah, it gave up on me years ago. I've been using a George Foreman grill ever since.'

'What about when you want something that isn't meat?'

'I just stick it in there anyway.'

'Doesn't matter what you're cooking?'

'Nope. Managed to rustle up an omelette in that bad boy the other day. Tasty.'

'You're a sick puppy, Banks.'

'Guilty as charged.'

I knocked his legs off the couch and took a seat beside him.

'So how'd it go?' he asked.

'Fine.'

'Lana try and talk you out of it?'

'I never said I was visiting Lana.'

Kirklander raised a knowing eyebrow.

'Fine. I went to see Lana. And yeah, she tried to talk me out of it.'

'She is wise as well as smoking hot.'

'Yes, she is.'

'I take it her pleas fell on deaf ears, hey?'

'Absolutely.'

'Good,' he said, clapping his hands together, 'certain death it is then.'

I nodded and pulled out my phone to send a message Cupid's way. Jamie Oliver was on the telly making one of his five minute meals. The cherub was banging on my front door before the fat-tongued chef had even had a chance to declare the grub "pukka".

'What do you know about The Tenth?' I asked as Cupid lit a fat cigar and settled into my armchair.

'A bit.'

Kirk waved him on impatiently.

'Oi, I work for her, not for you, ya great streak of piss.'

'Permission to kick him in his round little belly?' requested Kirklander, raising his hand like a schoolboy.

'Permission denied,' I replied.

'Aw.' Kirk folded his arms, eyeing Cupid evilly.

Cupid waggled a pudgy middle digit in his direction. 'Have one of these, you permed ponce.'

'Cupes. Focus.'

'All right, all right. The Tenth?'

'Yeah, any mentions pass by your ears?'

'Think so,' he replied, flicking some cigar ash into a discarded cereal bowl. 'Magic stone, right?'

'That's the one. I'm looking for it.'

'Why?'

'Because she is, dipshit,' Kirklander replied on my behalf.

Cupid blew some smoke in his direction. I snapped my fingers, interrupting their dick measuring contest.

'Do you know what it does?' I asked, bringing the conversation back on track. 'What The Tenth is for?'

'Not off the top of my head, no,' Cupid replied. 'Heard of it though. A whisper here or there. Important, I think.'

'Important how?' I asked.

'Buggered if I know. Fact I barely know anything about it suggests it's very important, though, wouldn't you say?'

I looked to Kirk, who rolled his eyes at me.

'That gross little goblin doesn't know anything,' he said. 'He's bluffing.'

'I know more than you, clearly,' Cupid huffed in return.

'Cupes, I want The Tenth. I want to know what it is, and I want to know where it is. Find out anything you can. Any-thing. Doesn't matter how small the nugget is, I want it. You got me?'

'Roger Wilco,' replied Cupid, firing off a sarcastic little salute.

His tiny wings fluttered and lifted him off the armchair as he readied himself to leave. He paused for a moment. 'Heard about Parker.'

'Already?' I said, my stomach twisting.

'Something like that? News travels fast. Parker was known. Was liked. A damn shame.'

'Yeah.'

Cupid nodded, then headed out.

'That must be the ugliest baby who ever lived,' said Kirk-lander. 'His mother must have shat him out.'

'Kirk?'

'Yeah?'

'Shut up.'

'Can do, babe.'

I had Cupid hunting for The Tenth, but that wasn't enough. I couldn't just sit around and wait to see what he managed to dig up. It might take him days to find anything of use, if he was able to find anything at all.

No, I had to do something, I needed to force the issue. In particular, I needed to connect with the most expansive information network in the Uncanny Kingdom: a species of information gatherers with the kind of investigative prowess that left Cupid's muckraking skills in the shade. What a pity they'd sworn never to help me after I accidentally-on-purpose caused a bunch of them to die.

Ilneer the eaves was sat in a corner booth in Baker's Pub, robed in shadow. He wore a knackered-looking grey trench coat at least a size too big for him, and a battered trilby squashed on his oversized head.

'Ilneer. Good to see you again, mate,' I said as Kirklander and I slipped into the booth opposite the reluctant eaves.

'Piss off,' he hissed, exposing a mouthful of tiny, jagged teeth that could slice through flesh like it was butter.

I once saw an eaves in a fight. He knocked a guy to the floor then pounced on him, gnawing at his face. Within ten seconds, all that was left of the bloke's mug was exposed skull and some tendons. Not to be underestimated, the eaves. Clever, but vicious with it.

'Aw, don't be like that, moley,' said Kirklander, reaching out a hand and sending ribbons of bright purple magic coiling around his fingers.

'Do not threaten me, imbecile. You or the Tattoo Bitch.'

'That's my nickname,' I said, leaning over to Kirk. 'Did I tell you the eaves have given me a nickname?'

'Aw, I want a nickname.'

'Will arsehole do?' asked Ilneer, lifting a half-drained pint to his thin lips.

Ilneer was the head of the Brighton eaves: a grizzled, take-no-shit sort who wasn't at all fond of me.

'You're going to help me,' I said.

Ilneer frowned. 'No help.'

'You're going to help me, and you're going to do it for free. No magic. No payment at all.'

The eaves leaned back in his chair and laughed. 'I fear Parker's death has broken your brain.'

I lunged forward, grabbing the lapels of his trench coat and yanking him forward. 'Don't you even talk about him.'

The eaves hissed, his teeth exposed, millimetres from my face. Clearly he'd have liked little more than to make me his lunch.

'Easy now, ugly,' said Kirklander, the ribbons of magic now forming a perfectly spherical ball of purple fire. 'Barbecuing an eaves would leave an awful stink in here.'

Ilneer closed his mouth and snorted. 'Let me go.'

I shoved him into his seat and sat back down.

'Why should I help you? Of all people, why would I help the Tattoo Bitch?'

'Because this means more than anything to me.'

'Sounds like a good reason *not* to help you.'

'It means so much, that if someone refused to help me, I'm not sure what I'd do. Not sure how far I'd go to hurt them. Pretty sure I'd make it my mission to kill them. To kill them and anyone connected to them.'

Ilneer leaned back, eyes hidden by the brim of his trilby, his mouth a grim line.

'Imagine it, Ilneer. Me and Kirk here, cutting and burning our way through the whole of the Brighton clan. Through every clan. City after city, town after town, wiping out every eaves who crosses our path.'

'I don't believe you would.'

I laughed. 'Maybe not in the past. But now? Now I'm not sure there's anything I wouldn't do. Not when it comes to this.'

Ilneer turned to Kirklander.

'Hey, don't look to me for help. What the lady wants, the lady gets.'

The eaves sat stewing for a moment, before standing and throwing his glass against the wall.

'Bit dramatic,' said Kirk.

'I do not take kindly to threats,' said Ilneer.

'Don't blame you,' I replied.

The eaves folded his arms. 'Before we would not help you, but after this? After this we are sworn enemies.'

'Fair enough,' I replied, getting to my feet. 'Now take me to your den.'

11

An eaves' den is a hidden place, disguised by strata upon strata of powerful magic. Not just any old concealment magic, though, the method the eaves employ to camouflage their dwellings is far more complicated than that. Instead of rendering their dens invisible like a regular wizard might, the creatures construct virtual mazes around them, building a bewildering labyrinth out of streets and doors that shouldn't join up with each other, but do. To find an eaves' den you need a guide, someone who knows how to unknot this impossible tangle of twists and snarls, and navigate the single path leading to the den's front door. In short, to find an eaves den, you need an eaves.

Ilneer led the way, with Kirklander and I hot on his heels. We followed the eaves down a back alley that took a sharp left turn that somehow deposited us on the roof of a tower block. From there, we chased Ilneer through a door that should have taken us to a stairwell, but actually opened out into an old opera house. A backstage door spat us out into the stockroom of a supermarket belonging to a chain that I'm pretty sure didn't have any branches in Brighton.

'You okay?' asked Kirklander.

'I'm fine,' I replied. 'Why do you ask?'

'It's just… well, you're sweating an awful lot.'

He was right. My clothes were sticking to me, and I could feel perspiration about to creep down from beneath my hairline and spread down my face. My tattoos really were on their last legs for me to be breaking a sweat during a light jog.

'I'm not sweating,' I shot back. 'I'm *glowing*.'

'Yeah. Glowing like a horse.'

I punched him in the shoulder.

On and on we went, barreling through a dizzying array of places, a disorienting jumble of disparate locations, until finally we stopped before the door of a large Edwardian house.

The building's outer walls were crumbling, seemingly only held together by the vines and vegetation that clung stubbornly to their brickwork. The roof sagged in the middle, its tiles sticking up in places like teeth in need of urgent dentistry.

'Nifty bit of magic, that,' said Kirklander, ignoring the den's aesthetic shortcomings in favour of its impressive security measures. 'Do you take commissions? I'd love to get something like that going for my apartment.'

'Shut up. Shoes off,' said Ilneer, opening the door and kicking off his boots as he crossed the threshold.

'Be careful,' I told Kirk in a low voice. 'Give them half a chance and one of these pricks will be gum-deep in our necks before we know it.'

We stepped into the house and took off our boots.

Time and neglect had performed irreversible deeds

upon what looked like a once proud house. The walls collapsed inwards, giving the place the appearance of a loaf of bread taken out of the oven too soon. Spiders scurried in dark corners, and water dripped lazily through gravy-coloured patches on the ceiling. Beneath our feet was a patchwork of random bits of carpet, which made the floor look like it had a bad case of alopecia. It's fair to say that the place wasn't exactly what you'd call prime real estate.

Ilneer waved us towards the kitchen, where another three of his kind were sat around a wonky table, drinking a foul-smelling tea and chewing on sewer fairies.

'What's up, guys?' Kirklander asked with a cheery wave.

The three eaves looked at him, each offering up a slightly different shade of, "Get fucked", face.

'Hospitable lot,' Kirk, whispered in my ear.

'What is it you want information about?' grunted Ilneer, now sat at the head of the table.

'The Tenth,' I replied. 'Heard of it?'

The pointed ears of the other eaves pricked up, taking in my words while acting like they were paying me no attention at all.

'Heard of it?' said Ilneer. 'I'm an eaves. Course I bloody have.'

'So what is it?' asked Kirk.

'Said I'd heard of it, didn't say I knew its shoe size.' He turned to his companions. 'Any of you lot know something I don't?' The eaves shook their heads. 'Oh, well, bad luck, we tried,' said Ilneer. 'See yourselves out.'

'Funny. I like you,' I replied.

'I hope you die soon.'

'All right, Ilneer, keep it light, will you?' said Kirklander.

'I want to know about The Tenth,' I said. 'I want your moley-looking kin to walk the streets, poke their noses in the darkest corners of Brighton, and sniff out anything and everything they can about that artefact. I want the news spread across the eaves network, right across the whole of the Uncanny Kingdom. I want it to be your personal mission to get me what I want.'

'That all?' asked Ilneer, regarding me stonily.

'You'll do it. You'll tell me what it is, and you'll tell me where it is, and then I'll leave. For good.'

If Ilneer was as well informed as he liked to think he was, he'd know enough about me to know I wasn't messing about. Finding the rest of the eaves' dens and making good on my threat to wipe them off the face of the Earth would be no mean feat, but I was a highly regarded killer, and connected to some powerful spell-slingers, including the great and mighty Carlisle. If Ilneer knew what was good for him, he'd do as I requested, and do it with a smile.

The eaves narrowed his eyes, his face twisted into a vicious snarl. 'Fine.'

The three other eaves blinked in unison like some creepy hivemind, then, without being asked, stood and marched from the kitchen and out of the house. They would hunt, and they would spread the word up and down the eaves' network. If there was anything out there to discover about The Tenth, they would find it.

As the door to the den slammed shut, Kirklander, Ilneer, and I sat in strained silence for several minutes. Kirk broke first.

'Anyone for a game of strip poker?'

Ilneer appreciated Kirk's stab at humour about as much as a mother appreciates the sight of a chalk outline on a crèche floor.

An hour passed, the three of us waiting and waiting and

waiting. By the time the little hand had made it all the way around the clock, I'd cringed to the size of a raisin.

Finally, Ilneer spoke. 'Must be hard.'

'What must?' I asked flatly.

'Your magic. It'll be gone soon. All used up.'

I felt my needles go up. 'What do you know about it?'

Ilneer smirked. 'Please. I'm an eaves, and not just any eaves. With Parker gone, your power is all but exhausted. We all know it.'

'I've still got enough juice left to kick your arse into an early grave.'

He grinned, showing me two rows of needle-like teeth. 'Perhaps, but not if you insist on running this fool's errand of yours. Seems to me you have a choice, Tattoo Bitch: waste the last of your power chasing an artefact that may not exist, or wipe us out while you have a chance. Because I promise you, once your powers have petered out, I'll make it my life's mission to see the meat stripped from your bones.' His piranha teeth chattered hungrily.

The cocky prick was practically begging me to kill him, but he was right. Even if I could wipe out the eaves, doing so would empty my tank, leaving me with nothing left for the Red-Eyed Man. I couldn't go to war with Ilneer and his people, at least not if they came up with the goods and sent me in the direction of the creature that took my brother. The rules of the game were clear. What we had here was an old-fashioned Mexican standoff.

'Maybe you should keep that dentistry hidden, pal,' suggested Kirklander, narrowing his eyes at Ilneer, his hand crackling with glowing purple juju.

'I can fight my own battles, thanks,' I said, cutting him off.

'Not for long though,' Ilneer replied in a sing-song voice.

'You're already looking weaker. Or am I imagining it? No, I don't think I am. All that magic that never belonged to you, drifting away, out of reach. Parker chained it to you like an unruly dog, and now it's going to jump the fence and go running off over the horizon, never to be seen again.'

It was all I could do not to hoist the kitchen table over my head and beat the smug git to death with it. Instead, I went to war with my words.

'I don't get it, Ilneer. You lot are supposed to be the best information gatherers in the Uncanny Kingdom—'

'Not supposed to be,' he interjected, '*are*.'

'Oh, I dunno about that.'

The eaves spoke through tightly-gritted fangs. 'What are you talking about, woman? Information is who we are.'

'Oh really? Only, it's weird, none of you little pricks has ever been able to figure out what happened to my missing brother. No one knows anything about a Red-Eyed Man, or the prophecy he's mixed up in.'

'That is weird,' agreed Kirklander. 'Hey, even *I've* heard of this Red-Eyed Man bloke. Me!'

I kept my eyes on Ilneer, steady and unblinking, watching for any tells, for the moment his body betrayed his intention to lunge at me.

'So what's that all about, moley? How come the great eaves' network knows diddly-squat about any of that?'

Ilneer smiled, but there was no humour in it. 'Who said we don't?'

The rest of the room had turned dark. All I saw was Ilneer. 'Don't bullshit me, you ugly little fuck.'

'Our lives are dedicated to gathering information; to listening, to storing, to knowing. We have no obligation to pass any of that knowledge on. Much of it—most of it—is passed only amongst ourselves. Just between our kin.' He chuckled. 'Some of the things we've kept close to our chests could alter the course of reality in ways you can't even imagine.'

My heart was loud in my ears. I think Kirklander was saying something, maybe trying to calm me down? I wasn't sure, I couldn't hear him. All I could hear was the eaves and that loud, loud heart of mine.

'Maybe,' said Ilneer, 'we know all about your brother and why he was taken. Maybe we always have.'

'Liar.'

'Maybe your pain and confusion and lack of hope are what keep us warm at night.'

The standoff was over. I swept the table aside and grabbed Ilneer by the lapels of his trench coat, my tattoos burning fierce, red light washing herky-jerk across the kitchen walls as we went to the ground and rolled over and over, fists flying, teeth snapping. An AGA cooker stopped our progress, and I found myself straddling the eaves, my hands wrapped around his thick neck.

'Tell me!'

Ilneer's elbow met my ribs and my grip loosened. The eaves bucked me aside and hopped up on his feet. I tumbled and mirrored him, crouching, fists clenched. He may have been old, but like all eaves, he was pitbull strong, vicious, and had a lifetime of fighting experience.

He reached into his coat and pulled out a knife that would have impressed Crocodile Dundee.

'It's time my kin were avenged for what you did to them.'

'Bring it on, Trick or Treat.'

He sprang forward with a low growl and I dived to meet him.

Only we didn't meet at all. Instead, we found ourselves

floating mid-air about three feet apart, unable to get at each other, our arms and legs swinging uselessly.

'Have you two finished, or do I need to put you both on the naughty step?'

Kirklander stepped into the gap between us, one hand extended, ribbons of purple magic rushing around and around it.

'Put me down!' I demanded.

'Only if you agree to play nice.'

'Fuck you,' I suggested.

'Now that doesn't sound like playing nice, does it, Ilneer?'

'I will cut your heart out, magician!'

'Okay, you're both annoyed at me. Some common ground to work with. This is progress, guys.' He clicked his fingers and a chair slid beneath me. With another sweep of his hand, I was gently lowered onto the seat, feeling every bit the admonished child.

He turned to Ilneer and extended his free hand. The dagger zipped from the eaves' grip and into his. He then tossed it into the air, where it blinked out of existence.

'That was my father's knife,' said Ilneer.

'It's safe and sound, I put it on the coffee table in the front room. Now, are you gonna behave yourself or what?'

Ilneer snarled, then sagged, nodding. The force holding him up let go, and he dropped to the kitchen floor with a wince.

Kirk put the table back and sat back down next to me as Ilneer picked up a fallen chair and sat.

'I would have taken the old fart easy,' I said.

'I know. But he wasn't wrong before, your magic is on borrowed time, don't be stupid and use it all up on him.'

I opened my mouth to tell him to bog off, but then

stopped and nodded. I knew he was right. I knew what was at stake, and I'd let anger overtake me anyway. Now I was calming down, I could tell that Ilneer had only been baiting me. He didn't have any secret information, I was sure of it. Well, as sure as I could be. Over all those years, something would have slipped. Hey, it was only in the last few years that the eaves had turned against me. What reason would they have had for not helping me before? I had the means to pay them, and that's all his kind cared about.

Before the terrible silence crushed us all once again, the front door opened and one of the three eaves returned to the kitchen.

'Well?' said Ilneer, drumming his long nails on the arm of his chair.

The eaves grinned. 'We have a location.'

I felt the corners of my mouth turn up. Finally, The Tenth was in my sights. Time to find out what it was, and what it had to do with my brother.

12

T here was a priest. Well, not a priest, not exactly. What's the opposite of a priest? If you said "tseirp a", go to the back of the class and eat ten sticks of chalk.

The priest's name was Neela, and she took the vows of the Antichurch aged just five, when the Great Finder visited her home, a shack in southern Russia. Right from the off, Neela's parents had known their daughter was different from their other children. For example, she'd been able to speak full sentences from the age of one, although, apart from, "I want food", or, "I want water", she mostly just repeated, "I am not yours, I am another's", which was a bit weird. Oh, and when she was baptised, she turned the water in the baptismal font jet black. Like I say, the clues were all there.

Neela was born to belong to the Antichurch, touched while she was still in the womb. But what exactly is the Antichurch? Good question, shows you're paying attention, keep it up. In answer to your query, the Antichurch is an institution devoted to the erasure of any and all religion.

Neela's parents weren't fully on board with this concept, but the matter was out of their hands. Once the Great Finder sniffs out a new antipriest, that child is removed from their parents and taken into his custody. He's not totally heartless, however. The parents don't live on in anguish, forever wondering what became of their lost child. Oh, no. He puts paid to that by chopping their heads off on his way out.

Wherever the agents of the Antichurch went, they spread doubt. They would seed confusion, make the devout distrust the stories they had been brought up on. They would enter places of worship and infect them with Nothing. A Nothing that would creep into the stone of the building, into its holy relics, its icons, and all who visited, all who came to pray, would feel it. That sense of emptiness. Of the Nothing. Of the absence of an afterlife. Of the lie of a loving God.

At any one time, there were three members of the Antichurch: a Finder, whose job it was to discover the next person born to carry on their hateful work, and two antipriests. The three walked the Earth, spreading their Nothing and infecting the pious with doubt. As you can imagine, this didn't make them particularly popular. A lot of people were gunning for the agents of the Antichurch, not least of all The League of Holy Assassins, who worked out of the Vatican. Consequently, the antipriests took to arming themselves against the forces of righteousness. According to the eaves who returned to the den with news, the antipriests had gathered many weapons for this purpose. Neela in particular was known to have filled her toy box with all manner of strange and deadly artefacts. And wouldn't you know it, one of those objects was a sliver of rock, about the size and shape of a wand. A sliver that Neela called, "Ten".

And that wasn't all. Rumour had it that Neela and her

fellow antipriest, Timothy (honest to God, his name is Timothy. He's from Birmingham, and he's mad about Led Zep) had been spotted, just a day before, in Bath, a city not far from Brighton. I mean, come on. It's as though it was meant to be, right?

B ath was a three hour drive from the coast. We took the Porsche there. I drove while Kirklander fiddled with the stereo.

'What did you do to my sound system?' he asked, exasperated.

'*Your* sound system?'

'This was my car before you stole it. You know, I'm still a little sore about that.'

'Your ankle, you mean? The one I broke right before I relieved you of your car keys?'

Kirklander huffed and sat back, crossing his arms. I sighed and placed a hand on his thigh. That perked him up a bit. Well, more than *a bit*.

'It actually does ache sometimes, when it rains,' he said.

'Aw, poor baby.' I removed my hand, much to Kirk's disappointment. No time for that. I changed the subject. 'Cool magic again, back at the den.'

'I know, right? David Copperfield, eat my arse out.'

'I think the saying is, "Eat your heart out".'

'I like mine more.'

I steered the conversation back on track. 'So, you still gonna pretend you got crazy good at magic overnight because you practiced a bit?'

Kirk was suddenly very interested in the radio settings again.

'You're keeping something from me,' I said.

'I might not be.'

'You're a terrible liar.'

Kirk sat back, running his hands through his thick mane of hair. 'It's just...'

'It's just what exactly?'

He opened his mouth, paused, tried again, failed again, then finally managed to string a sentence together. 'It's nothing. I wanted to improve, so I did. That's all. Promise.'

I trusted that promise about as much as I did the one I gave Lana about how I wouldn't die, but it was obvious Kirklander wasn't in the mood for sharing. Still, I'd get it out of him when the time was right. Because one thing was for certain, he sure as shit didn't get all Gandalf the Grey from a couple of weeks of book learning.

It was late afternoon by the time we made it to Bath, the sky just beginning to darken. We needed to locate Neela, and it didn't take a genius to figure out the most likely places to go looking. Kirk had his phone out, and over the next couple of hours we took a grand tour of the churches of Bath. Building after building was quiet, full of that held-breath atmosphere that churches seem to cultivate, with no sign of anything being amiss.

We found Neela in Bath Abbey, an Anglican church and former Benedictine monastery, founded in the 7th century. It had been built and rebuilt many times over the centuries, but yeah, basically, it was old as shit. A huge beast of gothic architecture that no doubt awed the holy hell out of everyone who saw it (at least before movies came along and really blew some tits off).

Right then, the only people inside of the abbey were me, Kirklander, and a tall woman in a long, brown coat. The woman carried a dark green leather suitcase, and wore her silken, black hair pinned up with a jade barrette, revealing a stark white neck.

She stood at the head of the church, eyes closed, her free hand resting upon the flat of the altar. No doubt a little of that Nothing she and Timothy carried around inside of them was seeping into it like strychnine, ready to poison the faith of anyone who came into contact with it.

I pulled a knife and strode towards her, flanked either side by rows of wooden pews, my boots echoing with each footstep.

'Yo, Neela, you interested in doing a swapsie?'

'Who are you?' she asked, her voice lightly flecked with a Russian accent.

'My name's Erin. Killer for hire. Howdy.'

'And I'm also here,' said Kirk, falling into step beside me.

'Sorry to interrupt you at work, but we're kind of in a hurry on this one. So, how about it? Up for a swap?'

Neela took a step back, her eyes flicking to any available escape routes. 'What kind of a swap?'

'Well, I hear from a pal of mine that you're in possession of all sorts of interesting doodads.'

'A pal?' asked Kirklander, cocking an eyebrow.

'Okay, "pal" might be a bit strong.'

'Enemy seems more accurate.'

'He's not wrong, Neela, that guy would definitely be up for a bit of dancing on my grave.'

'And pissing.'

'Oh, he'd empty his bladder for sure. Really hose me down.'

'Why do you both prattle so?' hissed Neela.

'Sorry, got off track,' I said. 'The swap, that's what you were asking about, right? Okay, here's the deal, you have a piece of stone that I'd like. That I'd more than like, actually.'

Neela hugged the suitcase to her chest, which told me loud and clear that not only did she have what I was asking after, but that it was on her person. Handy.

'It is mine. Leave this place, now.'

'You're not even interested in knowing what I'd give you for it? It's a hell of an offer.'

Neela shuffled, her brow furrowing. 'What would I get in return?'

I smiled, my thumb teasing the sharp edge of my knife. 'In return, I'll let you keep your life. I'll let you walk out of here not even a little bit dead. Pretty good, am I right?'

'You definitely come out of that deal with the better half of it, I reckon,' agreed Kirk.

'The whole not being dead thing is way better than having an old sliver of stone, ask anyone.'

'Fully agree. I'd hand it over without any nonsense if I were you, sugar. Best deal you're gonna get all week.'

Neela shook her head, her face twisted into a snarl. 'You will not take what is mine.'

'Is that the end of the negotiation?' I asked.

Neela threw open her coat and seemed to somehow *unfold*. She grew up and up, and out too, her torso widening, her legs and arms extending, hands growing big as wheelbarrows.

'I think that's a "yes"', babe,' said Kirk.

Neela screamed as extra limbs burst from her sides, thin and twitching and covered in razor-sharp spines.

'That is both impressive and terrifying,' said Kirklander, as Neela swarmed towards us like a giant, angry spider.

Great. A perfect end to a perfect day. Why had no one thought to mention that Neela was able to mutate into a massive, freaky monster? That's the kind of information that would have come in super handy before I went marching up to her with a knife and ultimatums. If I didn't know any better, I'd think Ilneer deliberately left out that bit of information. But of course I was just being paranoid, because if that *were* true, I'd have to wipe out every stinking eaves in the Uncanny Kingdom, and wear a smile while I was doing it.

'You run interference,' I told Kirk. 'I'll go for the suitcase.'

He nodded, planted his feet wide, and flicked open his long, ivory-coloured coat, ready, as I sprinted towards the rapidly advancing Neela with long, fluid strides.

'Let's have it then, you lanky bitch,' I yelled as my tattoos drew in power, drew in the old magic that drowned this ancient place. I felt fast, I felt strong. Jesus, I was going to miss that feeling.

One of Neela's gangly, barbed limbs struck out so fast that I barely saw it coming. I ducked and rolled out of the way as a blast of purple fire slammed into her side, knocking her off balance. Kirklander's work. She took her eyes off me as a second volley of magic began peppering her torso.

'How do you like that?' roared Kirklander, throwing way more style into his mystical gestures than was strictly necessary. It was more like he was dancing than fighting, the great peacock.

Neela still had a tight hold of the suitcase, gripped close to her stomach by one of the extra limbs she'd sprouted. I dropped to a three-point crouch, ready to leap up and make a grab for it, only to find myself flying across the church aisle as one of her free limbs swatted me aside. I crashed into the pews, landing in a heap on the stone floor, head buzzing.

'You okay?' yelled Kirklander, still fight-dancing.

I raised a hand above a shattered pew and give him a thumbs up. 'Okay, time to up the ant...'

I staggered up to see Kirk rubbing his hands together, summoning strands of magic that multiplied and coalesced, like he was swiping a stick around the inside of a candy floss machine. In no time at all, he'd fashioned a ball of magic twice the size of his head.

'Grub's up, baby.'

He threw it, and the magic struck Neela square in the chest. A scream erupted from her as the ball rolled around and around her body, stripping it of clothing, raking off whole sheets of skin. I figured that was her done for, but it turned out Neela was one tough, giant spider monster woman. Her scorched body bubbled and cracked, and for a second I thought she was about to crumble under the onslaught of Kirk's magic, but instead, a new set of limbs burst from inside her, making her even more fearsome than before. By the time she was done growing and mutating, Neela looked like she'd been bitten by a radioactive H.R. Giger.

'Holy shit, someone's had their Weetabix,' I gasped.

She scurried forward on fresh legs, eating up the ground between herself and Kirklander, eager to grab him, to tear him apart.

'Watch out!' I yelled, pointlessly.

Kirk didn't run. Instead, just as Neela was about to strike, he calmly leapt into the air, causing Neela to tumble past him in surprise. He landed in a superhero crouch, coat billowing, head down. It was impressive, I'll admit, spoiled only by the shit-eating grin he sported as he looked up to catch my eye. Okay, full disclosure, it didn't spoil shit. If it weren't for the fact we were being attacked by the spawn of the Devil, I'd have let him bang his wang in me right there on the church floor.

Neela righted herself and turned as I stepped in beside Kirklander.

'Pretty slick,' I told him.

'I'm very good, aren't I?'

I rolled my eyes. 'Okay, big head, let's finish this and get out of here. Do something to impress me while I grab that case off her.'

'Go get yours, babe.'

I kissed him quick, feeling hot, feeling so, so, sure of myself, then pulled away and ran towards Neela, knife in hand. Time to unleash the beast one last time. I called on my tattoos to give me power, to electrify my bones, to pump me full of rocket fuel...

And nothing happened.

I pulled to a stop as the adrenaline of the fight dipped away and the injuries I'd sustained flared up hot.

'Come on, come on, not now...'

I tried again, willing my tattoos to come to life, a sweat breaking out on my brow. My ink tingled and gave off a low glow, then bloomed bright again, flooding me with magic. Okay, it wasn't over. Not quite, not yet. The relief almost floored me.

'Heads up!' said Kirklander, then one of the giant, long, very, heavy wooden pews sailed over my head and struck Neela, sending her slumping to the floor, her myriad limbs twitching and thrashing.

She still had hold of the suitcase, but only just. I made a beeline for it, swinging my knife at a barbed limb that shot my way and sending a hose of blood spraying across a stone pillar. Another pew appeared above Neela, then dropped down on her, trapping her beneath its weight.

'No! It's mine! Mine!' she screamed, squirming, beating at the pew that pinned her down.

'Finders keepers,' I said, and swung my knife, slicing through the limb clutching the suitcase. I grabbed it, and the severed appendage flopped to the ground, dancing on the stone floor like a landed fish. I held the case aloft and showed it to Kirklander. 'Leg it!' I declared, but he was already one step ahead of me.

Kirk floated over my head, arms folded like a genie, moving swiftly in the direction of the exit. Smooth move. I began formulating some ideas about how I might make use of that little trick in the bedroom, then shook the thought clear as the pew pinning Neela let out a loud crack. Another couple of seconds and she'd be back up and ready to reclaim her stolen suitcase.

'See ya,' I called over my shoulder as I vaulted the pew that held her captive and sprinted for the exit. 'Don't forget to check out the Roman baths while you're in town, I hear they're a must-see.'

I had it.

I had The Tenth.

Now what?

13

It was gone midnight by the time Kirklander and I stumbled through the front door of my flat and flopped, exhausted, on the couch. I placed Neela's suitcase on the floor by my feet.

'I need a piss,' I said, ever the lady.

'Okay. Good luck in there.'

I stood and looked to the case. 'Don't open that without me, okay?'

'Scout's honor, babe.'

I walked to the bathroom as calmly as I could, trying to disguise how off I felt, trying to mask the queasiness in my gut, the spasms wracking my muscles. I closed the bathroom door, twisted the lock, and slid down the wall to the tiled floor, hugging my knees to my chest. I clenched my eyes shut and bit down hard on my hand, trying to ride out the crashing waves of pain that danced up and down my bones.

It was done.

I was done.

The way I felt told me everything I needed to know. My

magic, my tattoos, were exhausted. My body had rejected the last of Parker's ink. I was me again. A normal. Powerless, vulnerable.

I was scared.

I'd gone without magic before, but never for long. Even during those six months I spent in jail, I knew the situation was only temporary. At some point I'd be skipping down the steps of Black Cat Ink, ready to become me again. To become stronger than others, faster, more vicious, able to heal any unsightly wounds or broken bones I picked up. To be indestructible.

That was me. That's who I'd been since I was a teenager. It's what allowed me to do what I did. To become an Insider. To survive in the Uncanny Kingdom. And now... now it was gone. I felt like I'd been stripped naked and thrust into the wilderness with no way of protecting myself. No way of hiding who I really was beneath the tacked-on magic that was never really mine.

I rocked back and forth, pain rolling through me, almost making me vomit. How long would I last now? How long?

An hour and a half passed before I was well enough to unfurl my body and rise shakily to my feet. I took a look at myself in the bathroom mirror and found my eyes surrounded by dark circles, my lips bone white.

'You look how I feel, mate,' I murmured, then turned the cold tap, and doused my face.

I had to get a grip on myself. Yes, my magic was gone, but I knew that was on the cards. I was living on borrowed time now, but fuck it, I was still me. I still thought the same, still wanted the same thing. With or without my powers, going after James' kidnappers was a kamikaze mission, so what did it matter if I showed up without all the bells and whistles?

I grabbed a towel that should have been washed two months ago, and dried my face, taking a few calming breaths.

I was good. I'd be fine. Just carry on. One foot in front of the other.

I still had my own skills. My determination. With or without the ink, I was a vicious, nasty piece of work. Nothing had changed there. Whatever happened, I was getting my revenge. And I had Kirk to help me. Whatever he was keeping from me didn't matter right now. The fact that he'd mysteriously levelled up only worked to my advantage. I needed all the help I could get, and Kirk was willing to give it. To fight by my side. To fight with me. For me.

Unless...

'Fuck.'

I remembered the last time I let my guard down around Kirklander, when we slept together and I woke up to find he'd buggered off with the Soul Dagger and stolen a job from under me.

I tossed the wet towel into the sink and strode out of the bathroom. If he'd done it again, if he'd romanced me just so he could sleaze his way into my home and loot my belongings, I was going to have his balls. No, I was going to have his *head*.

I kicked open the door to the lounge—

To find Kirk fast asleep on the couch.

I let forth a long sigh. He'd stick by my side. He would, I was sure of it. It felt weird to be so certain, given our less than illustrious history. We'd fucked each other over so many times it was unreal. But still, I felt it. Felt it right in the pit of my stomach. He wouldn't run away again. Wouldn't double-cross me.

He wouldn't.

I grabbed the suitcase and deposited it on the coffee table. I looked over to Kirk, conked out on the couch, then popped the case's clasps and lifted the lid. It was packed full of stuff. A pair of shoes, a laptop, a pack of playing cards. I took them out, one by one, making little piles on the table.

Then came the other stuff. The artefacts.

There was a black skull, about half the size of a human skull. Stone? Marble? I lifted it out. It was heavier than it seemed, but soft to the touch. I tried to dig a fingernail into it, but couldn't break the surface. Soft but strong. Weird. I looked into the empty eye sockets and had the strangest sensation that something was inside the skull, looking back at me. Something hungry. I hastily put the skull aside.

Next was a knife. There's always a knife in these situations, isn't there? Its blade was metal, but starkly white. The blade was as long as my hand, heel to fingertips, with occult symbols carved along its centre. The weapon's handle was simple, carved from wood and wound with string that had been dipped in tar, giving it extra grip. I took out my own, shop-bought knife and compared the two. No contest. I tossed my knife on the pile of Neela's non-magical possessions, and slid the white knife into my pocket, wondering if it had any special properties for later discovery, or if it was just sexy looking.

There were two more objects.

The first itched my fingers to touch. A pair of wire rimmed glasses, their lenses as thick as my finger. Maybe Neela was just a little short-sighted or something. But that itchy, static feeling as I touched them, like thousands of tiny needles were pricking at me, was super weird. I shrugged and slipped them on. And quickly wished I hadn't.

All around me I saw half-formed figures, hundreds of them, squashed into every crevice of my little flat, their mouths agape. They were begging me for something, their eyes melting from their sockets, their shapes flickering in and out of existence. With a little yelp, I pulled the glasses off and dropped them in the bin. I had no idea what they'd shown me, but I knew damn sure I didn't want to see it again.

The final object was wrapped in a scrap of purple cloth. I unwrapped it to reveal a piece of stone, as long and as thick as a wand.

The Tenth.

I picked it up, passing it from hand to hand, running my fingers along its rough surface. I didn't get any sense of what it might be for. What it might do. Did it contain magic of some sort? I had to assume so, but what sort of magic, and how was it accessed? How was it used? It looked and felt just like an ordinary piece of stone to me.

'What do you think?' asked Kirklander.

'Jesus,' I cried, jerking to one side.

Kirk yawned and stretched. 'Well? What's it for?'

'I haven't got a clue,' I replied. 'Here.' I handed The Tenth over to him and he peered at it, stroked it, sniffed it.

'Definitely stone.'

'Well done, Columbo. Another case cracked.'

I took it back from him and slid it into my jeans pocket. 'We've got it, that's all that matters. We can get the rest when we meet up with your employer, that Chad bloke.'

Kirklander looked at me, his nose crinkled. 'Are you okay, babe?'

'Course. Amazing, as always.'

'Right.' He reached out, his fingertips dragging across the skin of my collarbone, across the faded shapes inked there. 'Are they…?'

I frowned and nodded.

'Shit.'

'Yup.'

'I mean, shit with another shit on top.'

'Agreed.'

Kirklander hugged me. 'How are you feeling? Really?'

'Like someone spent the last week beating me with a broom handle.' I wrapped my arms around his waist, and god dammit if the pain in my bones didn't cool off a little.

'It'll be okay,' he whispered.

'You think?'

'That was a clever lie to make you feel better.'

I laughed and pulled away, looking into his eyes. 'This doesn't change anything. I'm carrying on.'

'Pfft. So you don't have magic? So what? You're still the biggest bad-ass I know, babe.'

'Yeah, and don't go forgetting it, or I'll use your windpipe as a knife-holder.'

Kirklander winced. 'Jesus Christ.'

'A friendly warning.' I wriggled free of his arms, and shut the suitcase.

'I'm not going anywhere.'

'I know,' I replied.

'I mean it. You're gonna be the death of me, I'm pretty sure of that, but I'll be there. Next to you. Looking hot as shit while I do it.'

I smiled and just about managed not to thank him. 'Arrange the meet,' I said.

It was time to find out just what the Red-Eyed Man wanted with The Tenth. Magic or no magic, I was finding that motherfucker and making him dead.

14

Kirklander put in a call to Chad Bowles, his employer, who asked to meet him on the sixth floor of a local multi-storey car park. Which didn't sound at all dodgy.

'What's wrong with his office?' I asked.

'I dunno. Maybe his carpet's being cleaned.'

The plan was simple: Kirklander would go ahead, and I would follow on behind at a discreet distance, keeping an eye out for any nasty surprises. When Chad appeared, and if all seemed safe, I'd join Kirk and we'd get some answers out of the guy.

Easy, right?

Well no, of course not, it never is. I thought you'd have grasped that by this point. After all, I was going into this thing sans magic, armed only with my fancy new dagger. If the shit went down and I was injured, I was healing the old-fashioned way, which meant slowly and painfully, if I actually healed at all.

Fun, fun, fun.

Still, as I shadowed Kirklander, who strode boldly

towards the entrance ramp of the concrete eyesore that was Luxton Car Park, I felt good. I felt focused. I felt like part of a team.

The foot traffic was non-existent, Chad had requested Kirk meet him at one in the morning, so the place was a ghost town. The guy was really setting a mood. As Kirklander disappeared inside the car park, I dashed forwards and ducked behind the electronic toll booth by the entrance, scanning my surroundings for any sign of movement. For any eyes that might be trained on me. I couldn't spot any. Having determined the coast was clear, I glanced quickly into the car park and saw the hem of Kirk's coat flap disappear around a corner as he headed up to level one. I followed on.

Each level was empty for the most part, just a car or van dotted here and there. I did my best to avoid them. Each of the parked vehicles could have contained a lookout, someone to warn Chad that he was about to be double-crossed. Someone ready to hop out and slit my throat while I ghosted around, thinking I was being sneaky. You always expect the cold touch of a knife to make friends with your skin in this game.

'Hey,' said Kirklander, stepping out of view as he made it up the ramp to level six. 'What's wrong with the ground floor? You need to get your steps in or something?'

I crouch-waddled as far up the ramp as I could go without being spotted by Chad or anyone else who might be waiting up there. I peeked over a low concrete wall to see Kirklander walking confidently towards Chad, who was perched on the bonnet of an imported American car, some kind of Chevy SUV. He was clean-shaven and looked prepared, like he'd rehearsed this meeting methodically and knew exactly what its outcome was going to be.

'You got a problem with the way I do things?' he asked.

'Not really, just... a car park? Bit of a cliche, don't you reckon? I mean, where's your cigarette and fedora, Deep Throat?'

'You're the one wearing the trench coat, pal.'

Kirk chuckled. 'Touché.'

Chad stood, hands stuffed into the pockets of his bomber jacket. What else did he have in there? A gun? Was his finger hovering over a trigger, ready to unload a bullet into Kirklander's guts?

'You got the goods?' he asked.

'You know I do, brother.' Kirklander pulled The Tenth out of his pocket and presented it on his palm.

'Have much trouble getting it?'

'Nothing I couldn't handle. Fucking shit up is my meat and potatoes.'

'Give it over,' said Chad, removing a hand from his pocket and reaching out.

Kirk closed a fist around the artefact. 'Not so fast, chief. Time to pay the piper.'

Chad reached into an inside pocket and pulled out a fat envelope. 'Here.' He tossed it to Kirk, who reached out a glowing hand and froze the envelope mid-air, then drew it to his open paw like it was attached to him by a length of elastic. 'Impressive,' Chad admitted.

'It's a godsend when you've just sat down and you clock the remote control on the other side of the room.' Kirk looked inside the envelope, leafed through its contents, and pocketed it. 'Much obliged.'

'Now, the artefact. Give it to me.'

Kirk sucked in some air. 'Yeah, I'm thinking maybe I'll keep it.'

'What?'

'Yo, Erin, come explain to this guy why we think we should keep a hold of this rock wand.'

'It's not a wand,' I said, emerging from my hiding place and striding into the fray, my eyes scanning the shadows, ready for an ambush. 'Or is it a wand, Chad? You tell me.'

'What is this?' he asked, backing up a couple of steps.

'Other hand out of your pocket,' I demanded, gesturing with my white-bladed knife. 'Now, or I carve my name into a ball bag of your choice.'

Chad pulled a pistol and aimed it my way.

I cocked my head, trying to make out the model of gun he was packing. 'What is that thing?' I asked.

'Looks like 007's gun to me,' said Kirklander.

'Holy shit, it is. That's a Walther PPK. Man, I haven't seen one of those in years.'

'Stay where you are,' Chad demanded, his pistol visibly shaking.

I stood my ground. 'Chad, did you remember to shave the sight off of that shooter after you bought it?'

'What?' he replied, his eye trained on the pistol's aiming device. 'Why would I do that?'

'Because it'll hurt a lot less when I shove the thing up your arse, that's why.'

He made a face that seemed to say, *"It happened again. Bring wet wipes."*

'If I were you I'd listen to the woman,' said Kirklander, his hand beginning to glow with fierce magic, 'but in case you still need convincing, bear in mind that I know a little trick that'll make your head explode.'

'Do you?' I asked, stopping at Kirk's side.

'Sure I do,' he said, giving me a sly wink.

'This is bullshit,' spat Chad, placing his gun on the

ground and raising his hands. 'The deal was fair, you got your money.'

Kirklander spread his arms wide. 'Hey, didn't anyone tell you never to trust a killer for hire? We're bad news, mate. Especially me, I've double-crossed more people than I've had hot dinners.'

'I can vouch for that.'

Chad backed up a couple of steps, looking for a way out.

'Don't run,' I told him. 'If you run, I will chase you. Then I will catch you. Then I will knock all the teeth out of your head and make you swallow them.'

'You're making a big mistake.'

'Yeah, it's kind of a running theme with me. Now, I'm going to ask you some questions, and you're gonna answer them, got it?'

Chad didn't answer.

I took The Tenth from Kirklander and pointed it in Chad's direction. 'Why do you want this?'

Chad focused on the artefact, licking his lips. 'It is ours.'

'Whose?'

He smiled. 'Father is returning.'

'Your dad?' I asked.

He laughed and took a step forward. 'You understand nothing. And soon, you will be dead.'

'Big talk from a bloke who showed up to a shadowy rendezvous packing a peashooter,' said Kirklander, lifting a hand to show off the magical purple ribbons weaving between his fingers.

I fixed Chad in the eye. 'What is The Tenth? Why do you want it, and what's it got to do with the Red-Eyed Man?'

He grinned, sniggering, his eyes sliding from mine and back to the artefact.

I'd had just about enough of Chuckles. I slid The Tenth

into my pocket and lunged for Chad, gathering a fistful of his bomber jacket in my hand. I shoved him back against the Chevy and bounced his head off the bonnet, pressing the point of my new dagger against his throat. 'Unless you want that bollock signature we talked about, you're gonna tell me what I need to know.'

He didn't look scared. Didn't look intimidated. He just returned a dumb, lopsided grin. 'Father is returning. It's too late.'

'What's he banging on about?' asked Kirk.

'We are the Family of The Eternal. The all-consuming rage. The fire that burns all. This reality is a fraud, Father will return and he will burn it down to reveal the truth!'

I pressed down on the white knife, forcing a bead of blood to escape Chad's neck and slalom the stubble of his throat. He didn't flinch. His eyes were wide, his smile wilder still. 'Nothing will stop it. Praise the Family, for The Eternal returns. He returns. He has waited for so long. Praise the Father. Praise The Eternal! Praise the—'

He blinked, a look of confusion replacing his fanatical grin.

'Uh, you okay there, buddy?' I asked.

He was not.

His back arched and he coughed, blood erupting from his mouth as though his head were a volcano, splattering across my face, my chest. I reeled back in shock.

'What's happening?' asked Kirk, as Chad writhed and twitched and bucked on the car bonnet.

His hands clawed at his neck, his face. He shook as though he was having some sort of violent seizure, his whole body in spasm. Finally, he stopped and sat bolt upright. He looked at me, drenched in sweat, his neck and face covered in self-inflicted scratches, oozing blood.

'Praise the Father.'

'Chad, what the Dickens are you on about?'

He didn't get to answer my question. A second later, his entire body ripped apart as though some giant, invisible monster had torn him in two. The separate halves of Chad came apart like a meat piñata, spilling blood and slopping organs on the car park floor. It was... unpleasant. Don't get me wrong, I'm not the squeamish type—don't forget I started this story by sawing a guy's head off with a letter opener—but this was some next level gore. Honestly, there was so much blood it's like Chad's blood was bleeding.

'What...?' Kirk started.

'... the fuck,' I finished.

'He spoke too much,' said a third voice from behind us. A voice that sounded like an ill wind blowing through a field of tombstones.

I turned to see who had joined us.

A pair of burning red eyes looked back at me.

15

I'd waited most of my life for this moment. Ever since I first met him when I was just nine years old, I'd waited for the day I crossed paths with the Red-Eyed Man again. Now there he was. And I didn't have the slightest clue what to do about it.

The Red-Eyed Man was draped in a floor-length, burgundy robe with a hood, beneath which blazed two flaming red eyes. His body was entirely black, the blackest black you've ever seen, so black that it seemed to drink in all the surrounding light. I couldn't tell if he was dressed or naked, he was a strip of midnight in a robe.

He lowered one arm and the storm of electricity that had been dancing around it died; the power he'd used to rupture Chad's body and tear him in two.

I wanted to run at him. I wanted to run away. I'd dreamed of this moment so many times, asleep and awake. I'd fantasised about what would happen when I had the Red-Eyed Man in my sights, about what I'd do, what he'd do, what I'd discover. There were two main variations on how things would turn out: sometimes I beat him to death with my fists, other times he just laughed at me as I curled into a ball at his feet and wept.

Kirklander took a protective step in front of me, but I wasn't having that. I pushed past him and threw back my shoulders, defiant.

'Remember me?' I asked.

His eyes blazed even brighter, his blood red robe billowing in a breeze that didn't exist.

'I recall everyone who crosses my path,' he replied.

I could feel it. The power radiating from his black hole of a body. A powerful, old magic that ebbed from him, an aura that crept over my skin, that interrogated me, that filled me with a frigid, sinking fear. What was he? What could he do?

Kirklander coughed nervously. 'So who is it we're talking to exactly, Red?'

'My name is Scarbury.'

Strange. To have an actual name at last.

'The Tenth,' he said, his voice a cold shiver up my spine. 'Give it to me.'

I backed up, my hand instinctively going to the artefact in my pocket. 'Not bloody likely.'

Scarbury didn't react, didn't move forward to claim it. Instead, his aura intensified, pressing against me. It felt like hands squeezing my throat, digging into my windpipe. It felt like death.

'What do you want it for?' I wheezed. 'What does it do?' My heart was beating fast, my body shaking uncontrollably.

'So scared,' whispered Scarbury. 'So small you were. Small and frightened. You ran and ran and ran, even as I scattered your thoughts, your memories. Pulled the truth from you and released it into the wind.'

If he was trying to piss me off, it was working.

'Why did you take my brother?' I asked.

Scarbury's eyes grew so wide that they formed a single red light that filled the entirety of his face, then the light died down again, back to two burning eyes. 'Because we wanted to,' he replied. 'Because we could.'

'That's not an answer,' I said, pointing the tip of my dagger at him.

'A threat?' he replied.

'Of course it's a fucking threat. I'm going to kill you. What did you think I was going to do, buy you a round?'

His voice seemed to take on a smile. 'No. You will not kill me. That is not how it is written.'

My hand lowered a little. 'How what is written?'

But Scarbury wasn't interested in my line of questioning. Instead, he arrowed forward, his feet an inch from the ground, his hands outstretched. I dove out the way, Kirk leaping in the other direction, Scarbury missing us by inches. By the time I'd rolled into a crouching position, facing him, he'd already halted his forward momentum and turned to stare at me again.

'The Tenth,' he said. 'Give it to me.'

'Get fucked,' I replied, running at him. Stupid, reckless.

His eyes blazed brighter and I was lifted from my feet and sent tumbling head over heels into a concrete pillar. My head snapped forward as the pillar connected with the back of my skull, then I hit the floor like a stone.

'Not nice, feller,' I heard Kirk say, as I looked up, eyes blurry, the back of my head feeling like someone had sunk a pickaxe in it.

Scarbury floated slowly towards me, ignoring Kirklander, who pulled his hand back and unleashed a wave of fierce magic. Scarbury swept an arm in Kirk's direction, not only dispelling his attack, but smashing him into the side of the Chevy so hard that he totalled the thing.

I staggered to my feet, hazy, as Scarbury zeroed in on me, the air around him igniting, tongues of flame lapping at his body like hungry kittens going at a saucer of milk. I could feel the crackling heat on my flesh, ready to burn, ready to devour. I should have run, but I refused to turn tail. I wasn't nine years old any more. This time things were going to be different. This time I would stand my ground.

The Red-Eyed Man reached out a dark hand, his fingers curled into hooks, eager to close around my throat.

'Fuck you,' I screamed.

Thankfully, I had more than harsh words on my side. A second wave of magic struck home courtesy of Kirklander, catching Scarbury by surprise, and sending the bastard tumbling across the car park.

Kirk grabbed me by the wrist. 'We gotta go.'

I shook my head. 'No.'

I could see Scarbury collecting himself in the shadows. Rising, his robes billowing, eyes burning with fury, showering the ground with twin fountains of red sparks.

'He's going to kill us, you daft cow,' Kirklander cried.

'I'm not running!'

Kirk sighed. 'Fine.'

He wrapped his arms around me, then we were flying backwards fast enough to drag the breath out of my lungs. In less than a second, we were over the outer wall of Level 6 and hanging in the air outside. For a beat we hung there like a pair of Wile E. Coyotes, then we plummeted towards the street below, the world around me turning into a greasy smear. An inch from splattering on the ground, we stopped as though we'd landed on an invisible cushion. I wriggled free of Kirklander's arms and dropped the final inch, turning to him, furious.

'What are you doing?'

'Saving your arse,' he replied. 'Saving both of our arses.'

'You had no right!' I spat, shoving him.

A car to my left exploded, knocking us to the ground. It leapt ten feet into the air, a ball of molten, twisted metal, before crashing down again. I looked up to see Scarbury, still on the sixth level, glaring down at us with those blazing red eyes.

I jumped to my feet, grabbed Kirklander by the wrist, and we ran.

T he streets of Brighton streaked by.

'Have you got eyes on him?' I asked, the Porsche's wheels screaming against the tarmac as I took another breakneck turn, the back end kicking out, trying to drag us off the road.

'No,' Kirk replied, craning his neck this way and that. 'We're clear.'

'Are you sure?'

'Yeah. No. I think so. Who knows what that fucker can do? Maybe he's sat on the roof right now, enjoying the ride.' He slumped into his seat, facing forward again, a look of concern on his face. 'Are we cool?'

'Fuck you.'

'Is that your fun way of saying, "No"?'

'You had no right to do that.'

'Do what? Save your arse?'

'I'm not some damsel in distress who needs a big, strong man to save me.'

Kirk nodded. 'You think I'm big and strong?'

I noticed he wasn't wearing his seatbelt and seriously considered crashing the Porsche into a lampost just so I could see the look on his face as he went sailing through the windscreen.

'He would have killed you,' he said. 'Killed both of us, probably, though he didn't seem all that interested in me.'

'I've waited most of my life to find him. He was there. He was *right there*, and now what?'

'Now you have what he wants. Now you have some dirt on him courtesy of the late, great Chad. Now we use what we know to gather more info on him, and give ol' red eyes the worst day of his life.'

I gritted my teeth and slapped the wheel with the palm of my hand. 'Fuck!'

He was right. I knew he was right. God, I hated that. We were outmatched, what good would standing my ground have done us? Would being torn in half in a multi-storey car park have fixed any of my problems? I had to play smarter than that. If I wanted to uncover everything, if I wanted the truth and if I wanted revenge, I had to play this with a cool head. I had to stop being in such a rush to die.

'Thanks,' I mumbled, so quietly that even I barely heard it.

'Don't worry about it. I know all about the pitfalls of not thinking things through. It's sort of my speciality area.'

My phone buzzed. I pulled it out to read the message.

'More good news?' asked Kirk.

Cupid had something for me.

I took a sharp left and smiled as Kirk's face mushed against the passenger side window.

16

Cupid was perched on the end of the pier he slept under, absentmindedly strumming the string of his bow as he looked out at the waves, the whole scene flecked silver by a fingernail moon.

'Hey, Cupes,' I said, leaning against the railing next to him. Not so long ago I'd almost thrown myself off this pier. I shivered a little at the memory.

'The streak of piss still with you?' he grunted, not turning to look around.

'Yes, the handsome man who could crush you with his bare hands is still here,' replied Kirklander.

'Give us a minute,' I told him.

Kirk fired off a little salute, turned on his heel, and walked across the pier to take a seat on a nearby bench.

'You know, you could think about not giving him such a hard time,' I told Cupid, planting my arse beside him.

He looked at me, all innocent. 'Moi?'

I grinned and nudged him in the shoulder.

'Since when were you two a double act, anyway?' asked Cupid. 'You're always bitching about the bloke. Didn't you tell me once that you wanted to stick a gun in either end of him and pull the trigger on both?'

I looked out to sea, watching a gull sail high above the water. 'People change.'

'Not me,' Cupid replied. 'I don't even change my nappies if I can help it.'

'Yeah, well, what can I tell you? Kirk's really turned himself around lately. He's been loyal and he's shown he can be trusted. Plus, he bones like a total champ.'

Cupid grimaced. 'Is that what passes for romance these days? Jesus. Love used to mean something, you know, back when I was in the game. You should have seen it, Banks: wooing, courtship, nice clothes, everyone in hats. Now look at the state of the world.' He shook his head sorrowfully. 'Bunch of animals.'

'It's more than just a physical thing between Kirk and me. The fact is, I need him.'

'Because your ink's dried up?'

In truth, that was only part of it. Even if I did have my powers, I'd still have wanted Kirklander by my side. I didn't want to take this next journey alone. Maybe it made me weak that I wanted him there for support, but fuck it, if I was weak I was weak. Who gives a shit?

Cupid stopped strumming his bow and turned to me with his big baby blues. 'This ain't easy for me to say, Banks, but I'm worried about you.'

'You are?' I replied, touched.

'Course I am. We've known each other a long time, you and me, and... well, I'll just come right out and say it... you're the best meal ticket I ever had.'

I felt my mouth pucker into the shape of a cat's arsehole. 'Thanks a lot, Cupes.'

'Seriously, I mean it as a compliment. Without your

powers, I'm figuring you'll be popping your clogs any day now, and that's my finances all fucked up.'

'Is this going anywhere in particular?'

'Too right it is. See, I decided that the most important bit of information I could find—the thing that would help you, and, most importantly, help me the most—was finding you someone to replace Parker.'

I stood up, hands gripping the railing. 'What are you talking about?'

'Parker was a rare find, but I figured he couldn't be the only bloke out there doing the magic tattoo thing. There's a nail salon in London that does enchanted manicures, and a magic shop that'll do you pretty much whatever you like if the money's right. It stood to reason there'd be someone else like Parker juicing up normals, so I went looking for them.'

'And you found someone?'

Cupid turned to me and grinned, waggling his eyebrows. 'Oh, I found someone.' He held out his hand.

Without counting it out, I automatically reached into my pocket, withdrew a bunch of notes, and stuffed them into his chubby fist.

'Ker-ching,' said Cupid, stuffing the cash into his nappy.

'Well, who is it? Who's the artist?'

It turned out the "who" was a woman by the name of Madeline who worked out of a tattoo parlour in South East London. Woolwich, to be precise.

This news was especially fortuitous as I'd already decided that the next best move for me and Kirklander was to visit the city and drop in on Carlisle. That way, I could find out what he had to say about the stuff I'd dug up on the man I now knew as Scarbury.

I got to my feet and dusted down my jeans. 'Thanks for the tip-off, little man.'

'No worries,' Cupid replied, counting out the money I'd given him.

I turned to collect Kirklander and head back to the car, when Cupid piped up.

'Banks.'

'Yeah,' I replied, turning back to him.

'Give that red-eyed bastard one from me.'

I smiled, nodded, and made off down the pier.

T he morning sun was just peaking above the exit ramp as we pulled off the M25 and swung into London.

I couldn't believe my luck. Somehow, beyond all hope, Cupid had succeeded in finding someone with the power to make me Uncanny again. When it came to getting magic ink, I'd barely looked further than the door of Parker's parlour, partly out of loyalty, but mostly because I knew that artists with his ability were incredibly rare. I'd also heard that those willing to share that gift were even rarer, if they existed at all. Cupid didn't know for sure if this new artist, Madeline, would agree to refresh my tattoos, but he felt sure that I could, well... convince her. Don't get me wrong, I didn't want to threaten a woman into helping me out, and I certainly didn't want to beat the help out of her, but you'll understand by this point that I'm more than willing to cross the line so long as I get my way.

We parked up opposite Madeline's premises, a narrow shop with a black sign illustrated with a pair of crossed ink guns and the name, Ink Inc. It was six a.m. and the place was closed. Of course. Not many people lining up to get drilled by a tattoo gun at the crack of dawn. We'd have to wait until Madeline turned up to start her working day, and accost her then.

'What do you think he meant?' asked Kirklander, as I turned up the car heater and a Kinks song seeped out of the radio.

'What do I think who meant?'

'Chad. All that Father stuff. The Eternal. All of it.'

I shrugged and closed my eyes, suddenly feeling very tired.

'Can't be good, right?' he continued. 'Sounded pretty fucking awful, in fact.'

'Hey, feel free to run and hide if you're worried.'

'I'm not worried. Well, I am. Of course I am. Only an idiot wouldn't be.'

I went to answer him, but when I opened my eyes to do so, I found myself looking down on an empty crib. James' crib. You know when you know you're dreaming and you just decide to go with it? This was one of those times. I knew I was sat in a car next to Kirklander, waiting for a woman who might be able to make me special again, but there I was, in my missing brother's bedroom again, nine years old.

I turned to see Scarbury stood in the corner of the room, cradling James in his midnight black arms.

'Father is returning,' he whispered.

I looked down at my hands and saw I was holding The Tenth.

'Swap?' I suggested.

Scarbury shook his head. 'Both are mine. Both are his. The Eternal is waiting.'

'Who is The Eternal?'

James was crying. It was an awful, screeching, wounded sound. A noise that no living thing should make.

'Father is coming. For James. For you. For me. For us all. The fire of The Eternal burns bright today.'

...

An elbow in my ribs and my eyes snapped open. People were streaming past the Porsche on their way to work.

'Hey, sleepy head,' said Kirk, and gestured with his thumb.

A punky woman with cropped, bright green hair and black plugs in her earlobes the size of babies fists crouched by the shutters of the tattoo parlour, wiggling a key in the lock.

'Madeline?' Kirk asked.

'Matches Cupid's description,' I replied.

Madeline pushed the shutters up, unlocked the door to the shop, and disappeared inside.

'Come on,' I said, stepping out of the car and stretching my aching body.

We hustled across the street and pushed our way into Ink Inc. The parlour was cramped and long, more like a wide corridor than a room. The walls were covered in garish graffiti, with hundreds of tattoo designs and pictures of customers tacked all over them. At the far end of the room were two reclining chairs, awaiting customers.

'Not open yet,' Madeline called from a back room hidden by a black velvet curtain.

'Here for a chat,' I replied.

Madeline's pasty white face poked through the black curtain. Up close, I could see that her eyebrows had been dyed a shocking pink colour.

'Oh,' she said as she looked at Kirk. 'Oh,' again, as she turned to me.

'Morning,' I said, as brightly as I could manage.

Apparently, Madeline didn't like the look of us. She

stepped out of the back room, wringing her hands. She was wearing on oversized Bart Simpson t-shirt that reached almost to her knees. On her bottom half she wore leggings, covered in a burning skull motif.

'No,' she said. 'Nu-uh. Don't care who sent you. I don't do that. Can't even do it really, anyway. But definitely won't.'

'We haven't even asked you anything yet,' I replied.

'I know a couple of Uncannies when I see them,' she replied. 'Well, he is anyway. You are kind of. Sometimes. That's why you're here, right? It's you.'

She was clearly no dummy. She'd clocked exactly what I was after.

'I had a guy. He'd top up my tattoos every few weeks. Made me stronger. Faster. Helped me heal any wounds I picked up.'

'Then go see him.'

'I would, but he's dead.'

'Bummer. Still, not interested.'

Kirklander gave Madeline a smile that lit the room, and twirled one of the tattoo chairs in her direction. 'Please, honey, we're not asking you to do anything bad. She's trying to find her long lost brother and needs to be at her best. Come on, help a woman out? Sisterhood, right?'

Madeline frowned. 'You don't... you don't understand,' she said, fretting at her nails.

'Then tell me,' I said. 'Help me understand.'

'Maybe... maybe your last guy was good. Really good. Must be if you kept going back. But I'm not as good as him. I know I'm not. I can't control it properly.'

She looked up, her eyes wide, worried.

'How do you mean?' I asked.

She shook her head. 'It's just... it can go bad. I've seen it happen.'

Kirk pulled me aside. 'This sounds a bit iffy to me. Maybe we should listen to her.'

I looked back to Madeline, who seemed to have shrunk by six inches.

Okay, so maybe there was some risk involved here, but how bad could it be compared to the alternative? I was running headfirst into the worst situation of my life, and I was doing it stark bollock naked. Yeah, I had Kirk and his magic helping me, but I was still way too vulnerable for my liking.

I recalled the feeling of being stood in front of the Red-Eyed Man. In front of Scarbury. The power of his dark magic pressing in on me, charging the air around my body with pure evil. I was helpless before him, but I knew my path was going to lead me right back to the man. I needed some hope. I needed some edge. So, Madeline was a risk, but so what?

I took off my jacket and flopped it over the back of the tattoo chair. 'I'm going to try.'

Kirklander sighed. 'Of course you are. Since when did a dire warning put you off?'

'Madeline,' I said, causing her to nervously shuffle my way, 'we're doing this. You're inking me.'

'I can't.'

'You can,' I replied, cracking my knuckles, 'because if you don't, I'm gonna stop being so friendly. Understood?'

Her eyes darted to Kirklander, bugging wide.

'Hey, I'd do what she says if I were you. Got a bad temper on her, this one.' He turned the lock on the shop door, and Madeline sagged in defeat.

'Get in the chair,' she sighed.

I slipped out of my jumper and bra and settled down on

the leather seat as Madeline dragged over a stool and a trolley containing her equipment.

My eyes met Kirk's and he gave me a reassuring wink. Normally, with Parker, all I had to prepare for was a little pain. Okay, a lot of pain, but that was all. With this woman, I didn't know what I was in for.

'What's the worst that could happen?' I asked as she took up her tattoo gun.

'You don't want to know,' she replied.

Well, that's not ominous at all.

'Are you absolutely sure you want to do this?' she asked.

'Just get on with it.'

She sighed, then the needle started buzzing. Her skin began to glow from the inside, and she clenched her teeth, sweat beading her brow. A corona of fire erupted above her shock of green hair like a crown of flames.

And then came the pain.

The needle met my skin like a red-hot poker. My back arched so far I almost folded in two. This wasn't like with Parker. His tattoos hurt, but this? This was worse. So much worse. And she'd only just begun.

'I can't,' said Madeline, pulling the needle away.

I grabbed her wrist and pulled it forward with a shaking hand. 'You can and you will.'

'Fuck you,' she replied, then pressed the needle back to my flesh. I cried out as the world exploded and turned black.

'**W**hat did you do?' cried my mum, her eyes full of anger, of despair. 'Tell me what you did!'

I gasped as my eyes snapped open and I looked around wildly, trying to remember where I was.

'Whoa now, relax,' said Kirklander, his hand on my shoulder.

I winced and pulled away from him. I was still on the chair, but he'd dressed me.

'How... how long have I...?'

'Took her an hour to do the job. That was two hours ago.'

He held a cup of water to my parched lips and I drank greedily. I sat up slowly, feeling like I might collapse at any second. I stretched out my arms to study my new ink. The symbols were different to the ones Parker had favoured. I'd never understood how they worked, or what they represented exactly, but I'd become so familiar with them that they seemed something like a second language to me. These were foreign. Alien.

'Where... where is she?' I asked, only now noticing that we were alone.

'Madeline went to get some air and didn't come back. I'm getting the sneaking suspicion that she might give this place a miss until we're long gone. So... you're still alive, that's good.'

'Yeah.' Still alive but feeling like death. I took a breath and got to my feet, leaning on Kirk in case my knees buckled. They held. 'Did it work?'

'I think so,' Kirk replied.

I tried to put my new ink to work, to pull in the surrounding magic, to make it do my bidding. At first, nothing happened, then gradually, occult symbol by occult symbol, the tattoos began to glow. Began to soak in the supernatural radiation around me. I smiled.

'Bingo,' said Kirk. 'And to think you were worried.'

I raised an eyebrow dismissively.

It had worked.

Sort of.

The tattoos were glowing, they were pulling in magic, magic I could feel was available to me, but it felt... different. It felt wrong.

What had Madeline done to me?

17

There was no point in worrying Kirk. Sure, my tattoos felt a little off, but so what? It was a new sensation, that's all. Not necessarily bad, just different. It was to be expected, really. I'd only ever known Parker's ink, after all. His felt one way, Madeline's felt another. Nothing to get in a tizz about.

Okay, so Madeline hadn't been backwards in coming forwards with vague warnings about bad stuff happening if she worked on me, but I was alive, wasn't I? Alive and able to access magic, and really, that's all that mattered. I was no longer walking into danger with nothing but a sharp tongue for protection. I'd worry about the rest—whatever that "rest" might be—when the time came.

Until then, head down, keep moving forwards, assume all's well unless proven otherwise. Ignorance is bliss, right?

Okay, on with the mystery.

I needed to talk to Carlisle. Usually, he found me, or I'd strong-arm an eaves like Razor into getting a message to him, but neither of those options was available to me today.

Thankfully, Carlisle had recently provided me with an easier way to be in touch with him.

'Why is it always a sewer?' asked Kirk despairingly.

'Shut up and get down there,' I told him.

He sighed, hovered off the ground, and floated through the open manhole.

'Show off,' I muttered, as I gripped the rungs of a cold metal ladder and lowered myself down.

Carlisle had told me that the next time I needed to contact him I was to climb into the nearest London sewer with a piece of chalk. Why a sewer? Apparently, that was none of my business. He said all I had to do was scrawl *I Request Your Presence* on a tunnel wall, and he'd come find me. No clue how it worked. Sometimes, when it comes to things like this, you just have to shrug and say, "Uncanny shit".

My feet struck the slippery floor of the sewer tunnel. Meanwhile, Kirk continued to float, keeping his boots raised a good inch from the muck. Not a big fan of muck, Kirk. His flat was *American Psycho* levels of clean and orderly, whereas mine resembled the inside of a tramp's boot.

I rooted around in the pocket of my leather jacket, retrieved the nub of chalk I'd stuffed in there a couple of weeks back, and got to work writing my summons.

'How long is this going to take?' asked Kirklander, checking his white coat hadn't brushed up against any faecal matter, his nose wrinkling at the not entirely enjoyable stench that we'd dipped ourselves into.

'Don't know,' I replied, writing each letter nice and clearly.

'So it could take days for all you know?'

'Could be,' I replied as I hit the full stop.

'Great. Well, who doesn't love hanging out in a rat-infested tunnel built to transport shit and piss?'

'You think I want to be down here, Kirk? The last time I was in a sewer I was almost eaten alive by fairies.'

'Holy shit, really?'

'Yup. I'm telling you, the labours of Hercules ain't got shit on me.'

'Okay. We wait then.'

'Relax,' I said, 'it probably won't take long.'

Guess what? It took bloody ages.

Kirklander rustled up a sheet of cardboard that had somehow made its way into the sewer and unfolded it to provide a layer between us and the damp stone floor. We stretched out in the stink, listening to the sound of passing effluence, and throwing death stares at any rats who scampered too close.

'How is it?' asked Kirklander.

'You're gonna need to be a teensy bit more specific,' I replied.

'You know, the new ink.'

'It's fine,' I said, shifting uncomfortably, trying to ignore the fact that it felt like fire ants were nibbling at the skin my tattoos were inked on.

'I know when you're lying to me,' said Kirk.

'Says the guy who just "practiced" his way to a bunch of nifty new powers.'

That shut him up. Well, for a bit.

'I know people make fun of me,' he said.

'Everyone needs a hobby.'

He sagged his head. 'Everyone thinks I'm this great swaggering idiot, all mouth and no trousers.'

'Seems like you've got a bit more than mouth going on these days.'

'Exactly. And people know it. You can only pretend you don't hear your name being used as a punchline so many times before it starts to piss you off.'

I sat up a little straighter, hugging my knees. It seemed as though Kirklander was finally in the mood to talk. This was still fresh territory for the both of us. Sex and lies we had in spades, but sharing was for the birds.

'So you decided it was time to be able to walk the walk more?' I asked.

He frowned. Nodded. 'When I was a kid, about ten... that's when I first realised I had it in me. That I could do stuff. Magic stuff.'

'What was the first clue?'

He shifted slightly. 'I killed Stephen.'

'You killed someone when you were ten?'

'Stephen was my pet rabbit.'

I managed to swallow down an involuntary giggle, though not before Kirklander caught me and flashed a dirty look my way.

'I was trying to feed Stephen a bit of carrot and he bit me. Sunk his teeth in my finger right up to the bone. I've still got the scar, look.' He held his hand out to show me a small, white line on his right index finger.

'So you killed him?'

'Yeah. Well, by accident. I screamed when he bit me and all this.... stuff burst out of me. It was like a reflex. The shock of it popped the lid and magic poured out in every direction. Smashed Stephen to bits.'

'So what did you do?'

'I buried him in the back garden and pretended he did a runner.'

Kirk opened a hand and produced a ball of fire. It was

the size of a pinprick at first, but grew as large as a cricket ball.

'After that, I learned how to unleash the magic on command. It was easy, like clenching my fist. I assumed that was just the start of it. That my powers would keep growing and getting better, but they didn't. Always pissed me off, that.'

He tossed the fireball into the air and it transformed into a sleek, flaming dragon that wheeled around us a couple of times before guttering out.

'Yeah, well, look at you now, Mister Fancy-Pants.'

He smiled, but it wasn't his usual smile. Not the one full of spice and mischief. It seemed... tired.

'Come on, Kirk. You know you can tell me anything.'

The sad smile was replaced by a grim straight line as he considered my offer. Finally, he opened his mouth, only for someone else to beat him to the punch.

'You did not mention that you were bringing company,' said Carlisle, melting out of the shadows, sweeping his long purple coat and giving a brief, startling glimpse of the garment's inner lining. A lining that looked like someone had sewn real stars into it.

I pushed myself to my feet, annoyed that our visitor had cut Kirk off just as it seemed he was about to tell the truth. 'You took your bloody time.'

Kirklander stood and turned to the newcomer, all vulnerability gone now, his usual, cocky mask firmly back in place. 'So, you're the great Carlisle?'

The self-proclaimed rightful king of Uncanny England smiled thinly and bowed his head ever so slightly. 'The very same.'

Kirklander eyed him warily. 'Bloody hell, mate. I've seen dead Victorian orphans with more colour in their cheeks.'

Carlisle's smile melted. 'I suggest you keep your boy on a leash, assassin. I'd hate to see him take a fall into that river of sewage there.'

'All right,' I said, 'are you two ready to put your handbags away?'

Carlisle turned to me. 'You rang, I answered. Now, what is it you want?'

'I have something I need to show you.'

'Follow,' said Carlisle, turning and striding into the shadows.

'What is up with that guy?' asked Kirklander. 'Does he live down here, or does he go around all day wearing SPF 100?'

'Aw, don't be jealous, Kirk, it doesn't suit you.' I followed after Carlisle.

'I'm not jealous. I mean, what does he have that I don't? Apart from a lethal allergy to sunlight?'

As the darkness swallowed me, I homed in on Carlisle's footsteps and kept pace. My breath was a little ragged, which it shouldn't have been, and my skin wasn't just itching now, it was crawling. All along my arms and across my collarbone, like something beneath my flesh was writhing. I felt a strong urge to dig my nails into my tattoos and tear them free of my body. To make it so they weren't part of me any more.

What was I feeling? Maybe the graft had been unsuccessful, and my body was rejecting the tattoos. Maybe that's what I was going through. But no. I'd felt that rejection hundreds of times, burned out thousands of tattoos, and it had never felt like this. Never felt like my skin was some alien thing that was trying to slither off of me.

After a quarter mile of increasingly fetid tunnel, I found Carlisle stood by a rusted metal door.

'This your office?' I asked. 'Sweet. Cosy, plenty of shade, a nice view of the turd river...'

Carlisle shook his head. 'How is it possible that I have become beset upon by two troublesome women from seaside towns?'

'Pardon me?'

'Never mind.'

He opened the door and walked through. I glanced at Kirklander, then the two of us stepped in after him. Only we didn't step "in" anywhere. Instead, we found ourselves stood on the flat, concrete rooftop of the same building that I'd first met Carlisle as an adult. The place I'd confronted him with the revelation that the two of us had met during my brother's kidnapping.

'Now, where have I seen that trick before?' asked Kirklander.

'An old eaves taught it to me,' Carlisle replied. 'It comes in handy.'

'Eaves aren't generally big on sharing that sort of thing,' I noted, as Carlisle lowered himself into a green leather chair that was sat upon the roof. 'Especially not to someone as untrustworthy as you.'

'Oh,' said Carlisle, grinning wolfishly, 'even the most secretive of species will share what they know when you have your hands around their scrotum.'

'And did that eaves live to regret his indiscretion?' asked Kirklander.

'Who can say?'

'Well, you,' I replied.

'In that case, no, he didn't.'

I approached Carlisle and pulled out The Tenth. His eyes didn't move from mine.

'What is it you wish to speak to me about?' he asked.

'I've been doing some digging.'

'That sort of thing is liable to get you dirty.' Carlisle's brow creased as he studied me. 'Are you quite all right, assassin?'

No, I wanna slice my skin off. 'What? I mean, yeah. I mean, none of your business.'

He studied me some more, then shrugged. 'Okay then, enlighten me. What bone have you unearthed and padded into my kitchen with, all muddy-pawed?'

I told him what I knew: all the bits and the pieces I'd discovered since we last spoke. He almost seemed impressed by my progress. Almost.

I tossed The Tenth to him and he caught it without looking.

'What is this?' he asked.

'I was hoping you'd be able to tell me.'

Carlisle stood up from the leather chair and sniffed at the stone not-wand.

'Stone,' he said.

'Wow. So glad we came to you,' scoffed Kirklander.

'Please be aware how nice I am being by not tossing your companion from this roof.'

'Noted.'

Carlisle squinted at the stone, casting a scrutinising look along its length, as though he were a snooker player lining up a game-winning shot. He then tossed it from hand to hand a few times before bringing it to his mouth and giving it a nice, slow lick.

An eyebrow kicked up. 'It is a key.'

'You're sure?' I asked.

'Usually, and in this case, definitely.'

'So we just take your word for it?' asked Kirklander.

'A key knows a key,' he said.

'I have no idea what that means,' I replied.

'Consider me shocked. I have many strings to my Uncanny bow, assassin. One is the ability to create exits.'

'What about entrances?'

'Alas, no. But I find, on our shady side of the street, that an ability to create an escape route is much more valuable than an ability to gain access. A handy exit is what keeps you alive.'

'Okay,' I said, 'so it's a key. A key to what, exactly?'

Carlisle frowned. 'I'm not sure. Which is a rare and unpleasant feeling.'

He tossed The Tenth back to me and headed for the exit.

'Where are you going?' I asked.

'To speak to a man who would happily see me dead. Care to join me?'

18

I'd heard of Giles L'Merrier, of course I had. I don't think there was an Uncanny inside or outside of the country who hadn't heard tales of the great and mighty L'Merrier: the giant-slayer, the master of the black arts, the Merlin of our time.

Some claimed he was the last of the Originals, the very first wizards that had ever walked the Earth. Others scoffed at that, and said it was just a rumour spread by L'Merrier to make himself sound more powerful than he really was. Me, I didn't know which was true, but one thing I did know for sure: you did not mess with the fucker. Giles L'Merrier had more magic in his left testicle than most wizards would handle in their entire lifetimes.

L'Merrier worked out of a small antique shop in Notting Hill, just off Portobello Road. He rarely ventured out any more. Although he once took an active interest in the Uncanny world, and in destroying anyone with magic and bad ideas in their heads, he now preferred to sit apart from it all, not partaking. L'Merrier had become a rock in a stream, resisting the water's flow, holding fast against the rapids. It's been said that many have tried to pull L'Merrier back into the Uncanny world over the years, to convince him to fight for their cause, and each of them had suffered his wrath. Rumour had it that one man had merely asked an opinion of the wizard, and lost his head for the trouble. So this was gonna go great.

'Why does L'Merrier wanna snuff you out?' Kirklander asked Carlisle as we paused at the end of the street housing L'Merrier's Antiques. 'Not that I blame the guy, you give off a real snuffable air.'

'A man can judge his worth by the strength of his enemies,' replied Carlisle. 'I count some of the greatest magicians born to the Uncanny world, not to mention fallen angels, amongst mine.'

'Okay, show off,' Kirk replied.

'Come,' said Carlisle, striding towards the shop. We went to follow, but Carlisle raised a hand. 'The idiot stays where he is. Two uninvited guests is quite enough.'

Kirk turned to me for support, but I just shrugged.

'You heard the man.'

'Since when was pasty in charge?'

I took Kirklander to one side. 'Look, L'Merrier is his guy, he knows how to play him. And besides, I need Carlisle on my side.'

'Why do you?'

'Because he was there when James was taken, and he's just as eager to find out what happened that night as I am.'

Kirklander frowned and squinted after Carlisle. 'I don't trust him.'

I cupped his face and turned him back to me. 'Then trust me, okay?'

Kirk huffed, then softened. 'Fine. I'm going to get a

Coke.' He kissed me on the point of my nose, cast one last evil look Carlisle's way, then left in search of a fizzy drink.

I caught up to Carlisle just as he arrived in the doorway of L'Merrier's Antiques. The shop's wooden sign swung overhead, creaking back and forth on the breeze. I tried to peer through the thick glass of the shop's window to see inside, but it was too milky with grime for me to penetrate. No, not grimy... it was as though the glass was made of some shifting fog. No matter how closely I looked, all I could make out of the shop interior were the vaguest of fuzzy shapes.

'So what's the plan here?' I asked. 'Far as I've heard, this guy isn't down for a stop and chat.'

'Leave the talking to me,' replied Carlisle. 'I can handle L'Merrier. You just stay out of the way and don't touch anything.'

'Why does he want you dead, anyway?'

'I have given him many good reasons over the years.' He looked at me, his dark eyes twinkling. 'I have had some fun in my time.'

As I looked into the darkness of his eyes, I imagined I could see faces, screaming, being cleaved in two, stomped upon. I imagined fires raging and hearts breaking. Flesh tearing and bones snapping. At least... I think I imagined them.

I pulled back, blinking, feeling like my eyeballs needed a good bleach. 'What was that?'

'That,' he replied, 'was fun.'

He pushed open the door and stepped into the shop, setting a miniature bell tinkling. I shuddered slightly and followed him inside.

L'Merrier's Antiques was thick with dust and crowded with shelves and objects. As a matter of fact, the inside of the shop was so thick with dust that it felt like I was walking through the ashy aftermath of a volcanic eruption.

'Bloke could use a cleaner,' I said, trying not to launch into a coughing fit.

The shop was packed to the rafters with objects of all shapes and sizes: antique furniture, rare knick-knacks, ancient heirlooms, animal skulls, suits of armour. In some respects, the place looked like an ordinary, ramshackle antique emporium, but I suspected that the things this shop housed were not your everyday bits of old tat. Each of the objects on display had some connection to the Uncanny. Each was the subject of a campfire story that had been shared for generations.

Carlisle gestured towards a spear blanketed in a layer of dust as thick as your thumb. The weapon's bent, blunted head was supported by a metal staff fashioned to resemble a gnarled branch. 'Once upon a time, that weapon was used by a high demon to fell angels during the first celestial war.'

'The first what?'

Carlisle tutted and shook his head. 'Kids today.'

I winced. Nothing to do with Carlisle, just a sudden wave of nausea as I was struck by a pain that felt like ragged fingernails being dragged across my tattoos. Across open wounds.

'What is wrong?' asked Carlisle, observing my discomfort.

'Nothing. I'm fine.' I straightened up and did my best to push the pain to the back of my mind. 'So where is he? Where's the mighty L'Merrier?'

'He knows we're here,' he said. 'He knew the moment we arrived upon this street that he had visitors. He just likes to keep people waiting. Just one of his many irritating habits.'

'You seem pretty sure this guy hates you. What makes you think he'll help?'

Carlisle clapped his hands together and shouted into the shadows. 'Magician, you have customers. Come out, come out, you engorged charlatan.'

Poking a bear that's already pissed off at you didn't seem the wisest course of action to me, but hey, what do I know?

'Carlisle,' uttered a booming voice that rolled out of the darkness like a velvet carpet.

'Always lurking in the shadows, L'Merrier,' said Carlisle, 'hiding like a cockroach, scurrying from the light, chased into a crevice by a housemaid's broom.'

The darkness seemed to part and a figure drifted forward into the light. Not walked, drifted. He was a great fist of a man, mounds of solid fat covered in a floor-length, scarlet robe. His head was a cueball, and his eyes looked like they could cut you in two with a single glance.

'You would do well not to test me, sewer born,' rumbled Giles L'Merrier. 'The only reason you live at all is because I allow it to be so. Your continued existence is a debt you cannot hope to repay. For my kindness, you should be lavishing my feet daily with kisses.'

Carlisle smiled and bowed slightly. 'I am ungrateful, it is true. I believe it to be one of my finer qualities.'

A smile flickered across L'Merrier's face, so brief that I questioned whether it had really happened. I was beginning to get the distinct impression that these guys enjoyed their mutual animosity. In fact, the way they were carrying on, it was hard to tell whether they wanted to kill each other or tear one another's clothes off.

'And who is this scrap of skin insulting my shop with her presence?' asked L'Merrier, turning his attention to me.

'You talking about me, tubs?' I replied.

Carlisle stepped in front of me as the air around the great, rotund wizard blackened and began to crackle with unholy magic. 'L'Merrier, I came to you looking for answers,' stated my companion, holding a hand out defensively.

The magic puttered out as L'Merrier's attention was snatched away. 'Ah. Something you do not know that you wish me to enlighten you about?'

'Indeed,' Carlisle confessed.

'Why does your lack of knowledge not surprise me?' L'Merrier replied with a wry chuckle. 'No one with the stink of the sewer in his bones could possibly be expected to be a scholarly man. What would you know of the written word, Carlisle, save for the occasional scrap of discarded newspaper that might wash down a drain and find its way to your septic domain?'

'I'll have you know that I have studied in some of the finest educational institutions in the Uncanny Kingdom,' said Carlisle, buffing his nails on the lapel of his purple coat.

'Nonsense,' L'Merrier snorted. 'Why, any learned man worth his salt would run screaming from such malodorous vermin as yourself.'

'And yet there you stand,' said Carlisle, and the two of them exchanged another look that told me their hostile words were little more than a veneer to conceal a mutual sense of admiration. And quite possibly, sexual attraction.

One thing I was sure of was that Giles L'Merrier was incredibly full of himself (and at least six other people, judging by the size of him). I shook my head. Just when you think you've met the most pompous wizard in London, along comes another one to put him in the shade (and a whole lot of shade, too).

L'Merrier waved a pudgy hand at Carlisle, beckoning

him forward. Carlisle hesitated, then took the bait. Despite his considerable ego, it seemed to me that Carlisle was actually a little afraid of the fat magician.

'Speak to me, shit stain,' said L'Merrier. 'Perhaps if I find your words intriguing enough I will let you walk out of my shop with both of your hands still attached.'

'Tell me, L'Merrier, what do you know of The Tenth?'

Carlisle's words hung in the air for several seconds as L'Merrier's eyes grew wide. If this was poker, I'd be tossing my hand aside already.

'Why do you ask about this object?'

'Because I and my assassin friend here have been asked to recover it,' he lied.

'By whom?'

'I'm afraid criminal/employer confidentiality dictates that I keep such information to myself.'

L'Merrier steepled his fingers and rested his hands on top of his great hill of a stomach. 'Why do you come to me?'

'Because I like to know what I'm getting into. I do not know what this object is, and I do not like not knowing things.'

'You intend to find it?'

'I do.'

L'Merrier frowned. 'It is a key.'

'A key to what?' I asked.

Carlisle turned to me fiercely. 'Hush, assassin.'

'All right, moody bollocks.'

'What is a key for?' asked L'Merrier.

'To turn a lock.'

He spread his arms wide and smiled.

'And what's behind the lock?' I asked.

L'Merrier drifted to a shelf, his hand brushing lightly

across the objects stored there, his back to us. 'What do you know of.... The Eternal?'

Chad had mentioned something about The Eternal, but only obliquely, and mixed in with a whole load of other word salad that meant fuck all to me.

'I know some,' replied Carlisle, possibly bluffing, it was hard to tell.

'Clearly not enough, or we would not be limping through this tiresome meeting.'

'Then enlighten me.'

L'Merrier drew a long, impatient breath. 'There was a creature, many thousands of years ago. A creature made of magic. Of great power. Of pure evil. It strode across continents leaving death and destruction in its wake.'

'There seem to be many creatures of this ilk,' replied Carlisle, unimpressed.

L'Merrier turned. 'Not like this. Not like The Eternal.' He lowered his eyes for a moment as if looking into the past, then carried on. 'An army of witches and wizards banded together, forming a coalition, an opposing force to do battle with The Eternal. It was a battle that ruptured landmasses. That cut down mountain ranges and parted oceans. Eventually, The Eternal was pushed back. Was forced into a realm separate from our own. A lock was placed over the entrance of this realm to ensure that The Eternal could never find his way back to ours.'

'Where is this lock?' asked Carlisle.

'You would most likely know it as Stonehenge.'

'No fucking way,' I said.

'There are ten keys needed to open the door. All ten were scattered across the realms, their locations concealed so that no one would ever be able to open the henge and give The Eternal access to our world.'

'So The Tenth is key number ten?' said Carlisle.

L'Merrier clapped his hands sarcastically. 'Very good, sewer born. Have a biscuit.'

'Hey, don't get all snotty with him,' I said, feeling suddenly defensive of Carlisle.

L'Merrier narrowed his eyes at me. 'Who are you working for, woman?'

'It's like the man says, that's confidential.'

The fat wizard grimaced, then shook his head. 'Do not continue along this path. Both of you. Kill whoever hired you, and if somebody hired them, kill them, too.'

'Seems a bit much.'

'You do not understand. This path must not be walked. If you dare carry on, you will be tempted by all sorts of wealth, of power beyond all reason. Do not allow temptation to lead you by the nose. The keys must remain lost. The lock must never be turned. Do you understand? Your lives depend on it. All of our lives do.'

19

With Giles L'Merrier's warning still ringing fresh in our ears, we collected Kirklander and headed for The Beehive, a pub in Ealing Broadway that catered to Uncanny types.

The Beehive was a musty, old-fashioned boozer with weathered furniture, an open fireplace, and mangy mutts parked under tables occupied by grizzled, shifty-eyed ne'er-do-wells. The locals were a rum lot indeed: a gaggle of rogues and vagabonds of all shapes and sizes. At a glance, I made out a cyclops, some kind of reptile creature, and what was either a werewolf stuck mid-change, or a very hairy man.

The three of us weaved our way to the bar and ordered a round of drinks from a landlord so tall it looked like he'd been stretched out on a medieval rack. While we waited for our beers to arrive, I looked behind the bar and saw a sign on the wall that read:

No Children
No Magic

No WiFi

We paid for our drinks, found a sticky booth at the back of the saloon, and settled in.

'Why didn't you tell L'Merrier we already have The Tenth?' Kirk asked Carlisle.

'Because I like to know what I'm holding before I play my hand, you waste of a haircut.'

Kirk went to respond with something pithy, but settled on sulking into his pint.

I reached across the table to grab my beer and it felt as though my skin was tearing. Somehow, I managed to bite down on the pain, and froze as I waited for it to subside. It was getting worse. Whatever Madeline had done to me, it was getting to be unbearable.

'The stuff L'Merrier told you sounds, you know, on the shit side of bad,' said Kirklander, taking a sip of his pint.

I nodded and slowly lifted my drink to my lips. The beer hit the back of my throat like a blessing, the ice-cold liquid quenching the fire that had taken up residence in my body. I sighed with relief, the feeling practically orgasmic.

'L'Merrier is known to exaggerate,' replied Carlisle.

'And is he this time?' I asked.

'No.'

'Great. So Scarbury, the Red-Eyed Man, whatever you want to call him, is working towards freeing this Eternal bloke. Or "Father", as the late, great Chad called him, God rest his exploded soul.'

'It would seem so,' replied Carlisle.

'And for some reason, tied into the whole thing, there's the kidnap of my baby brother.'

'Indeed, that part is a puzzle,' said Carlisle.

I slumped back in exasperation. 'Why is it that with

every new piece of information we get, the picture only gets more fucked?'

'Maybe we should do what L'Merrier said,' whispered Kirklander.

'Do what now?'

'I mean, the guy was pretty strong on this, babe. We're heading towards a steaming pile of shit, maybe we should take a swerve. Toss The Tenth and bury it some place deep.'

'Are you kidding me? What about James? You can walk away if you like, but I can't. I won't!'

Kirklander held up his hands calmingly, the way a zookeeper trapped in a cage with a wild gorilla might. 'Hey, I know, I was just thinking a few cowardly thoughts out loud, that's all.'

I felt a flush of relief. 'So you'll stay.'

'Seems that way,' replied Kirk. 'You know, I'm getting kinda nostalgic for a time when my conscience kept its mouth shut and let me run away from things.'

I grinned and nudged him with my shoulder.

'You two are making my teeth hurt,' said Carlisle sourly.

Like I cared. I slapped my palms down on the table and rose to my feet. 'Right then, I'm off for a piss.'

Carlisle's lip curled. 'Please do keep us informed of all of your toiletry intentions from now on, I'd hate to be kept in the dark.'

I downed the last of my pint and headed across the straw-strewn floor to the Ladies. It was as I was washing my hands in the sink that things took a nosedive. Ever since Madeline gave me my tattoos, I'd been feeling steadily worse. Pain, sickness, trembling; my back had felt clammy for hours now. But as I ran my hands under the hot tap, things leapt up about six notches.

It started as a whisper in my ear. Only it wasn't in my ear

at all, the voice was inside my head. A distant murmur I couldn't quite make out, words spoken in some faraway place. Too late, I realised I was lying on the filthy bathroom floor, curled up on my side, clutching my knees to my chest. I don't remember how I got there. One moment I was giving my hands a rinse, then the film skipped forward and I was horizontal.

The flesh on the backs of my arms rippled. It felt like there were bugs under my skin, trying to escape, trying to gnaw free of my insides. Repulsion gripped me. Madeline's ink, her magic, hadn't grafted to my body, it had opened a hole that had let something in. Something dark. Something rotten. Something that wanted to claim me as its own.

I realised I was screaming, thrashing around on the floor like I was having a fit. Maybe I *was* having a fit. I scratched at my arms, my shoulders, my collar bone. 'Off! Get it off! Get it off!' My fingers were wet with blood.

'Ours, ours, ours, ours,' whispered the voice in my head, clearer now. Only it wasn't one voice, it was ten, twenty, thirty, all saying the same thing, over and over.

The last thing I saw before I passed out were what looked like fingers, reaching out from inside my shredded arm, trying to push through the skin and escape.

***

P assing out had been a relief. A relief I didn't expect to wake up from. But wake up I did.

My eyes creaked open, sticky with sleep. I was woozy, the world around me glazed in syrup.

'You are alive,' came a voice. Carlisle.

'Wh-where are we?' I asked, the room around me starting to sharpen.

I was in a small bedroom. Bare floorboards, a large wardrobe, no windows. I was laid out on a single, metal-framed bed. Carlisle was sat on a simple wooden stool at my bedside.

'A property of mine,' he replied. 'I keep quarters all over the city. I believe it unwise to call any one place home, and certainly not when you are as dastardly as I.'

'Where's Kirk?' I asked.

'Running an errand.'

'I can't feel anything,' I said, and I was telling the truth. From the neck down I had zero physical sensation. I was, to all intents and purposes, paralysed.

'My doing,' replied Carlisle.

'Why?'

He didn't need to answer. I looked down and immediately wished I hadn't. Have you ever seen *The Thing*? That '80s Kurt Russell horror film? In it, there's this alien that can turn into anything. Can take on any form. While it's changing, though, it looks gross. I mean, *really* gross. Imagine warped, melted flesh with limbs and mouths and all sorts of junk jutting out of it at crazy angles. Got it? Well, that should give you some idea of what I looked like from the neck down.

I think I screamed. I think I screamed a lot. I can't be sure, as for a few seconds, I took total leave of my senses.

Carlisle shook his head. 'Oh, hush. Don't be such a drama queen.'

'What's happening? What's happening?' I tried not to look down but I couldn't help myself. Couldn't help but stare in horror at my deformed, broken body. At the leering faces pressing out from inside of my stomach. At the alien hands reaching out of my arms, branching out from my own limbs like the boughs of a tree.

'It would appear that you have an infection,' Carlisle replied matter-of-factly.

'A pretty fucking bad infection!' I cried.

'The woman who tattooed you, your coiffured companion said she warned you that things might not go according to plan.'

'She said it could go bad, but nothing like... this.'

I caught sight of the three faces pressing out of my torso, their mouths forming silent screams.

'Don't worry, I muted them,' said Carlisle. 'They enjoy talking about themselves even more than Giles L'Merrier does. Tiresome demons.'

'Demons?'

'Of a kind. A lowly, dreadful kind.'

'Madeline put demons in me?'

'It seems she is not entirely in control of her power.'

'You think?'

Carlisle narrowed his eyes at me. 'Magic is a delicate art. You cannot just haphazardly etch it into the flesh of someone not born to the Uncanny and trust that all will be well. Your friend Parker knew this. It takes artistry to perform such a feat, an exceptional degree of control. I myself would not be able to do it, and I am Carlisle.'

'So Madeline makes a balls of it, and a bunch of demons set up shop inside of me?'

'Consider yourself lucky it is more than just one.'

'Oh sure, lucky old me.'

'If it had only been one demon, you would no doubt already be dead. It is only because she got it so very, very wrong that several low-level demons were able to gain access, and are now squabbling inside of you like children, arguing over whose turn it is to play with the best toy.' Carlisle reached into a pocket of his purple coat and plucked out a paperback of Stephen King's *Pet Semetary*. He opened it, crossed his legs, and began flicking through the book.

'What are you doing?'

'It is called reading. You might consider trying it one day.'

I couldn't believe it. There I was, bursting at the seams with demons, and Carlisle was catching up on a spot of light reading like he was sat in a cafe, whiling away a rainy afternoon.

'Get these fuckers out of me,' I cried.

'I cannot. The only way I can assist you is if your snivelling lapdog locates the poor excuse for a tattoo artist whose services you procured, and brings her here. That's assuming he isn't busy with a hair appointment.'

'And if Kirk can't find her?'

'Don't worry, I won't allow you to suffer. I'll break your neck.'

'Great. That's calmed me right down, that has.'

Carlisle shrugged and returned to his book. Meanwhile, I closed my eyes and tried to pretend I was somewhere else. Anywhere else. I went to lots of different places. Happy places. I went to my bedroom and rode Kirklander like a rodeo cowboy. I went to Gjindor's demonic realm and slayed him dead. I went to my childhood home and killed the ever-living fuck out of Sharez Jek. I went to my mum's hospital bed as a child and saw my baby brother for the very first time, swaddled in a blanket, pristine, perfect.

My reverie was interrupted by the sound of boots clattering on floorboards.

'Holy fuck on a fuckstick,' said Kirklander, laying eyes on me.

'Yes,' agreed Carlisle, 'her condition has progressed a touch.'

'Hey,' I said, relieved to see Kirk back, and dragging behind him a terrified, green-haired woman. 'Madeline, you absolute bastard, look what you did to me.'

'I-I warned you. I did. It's not my fault.'

Kirklander yanked Madeline forward and she dropped to her knees like a James Brown closer. She was in a bad way, shaking and crying, but I can't say I was feeling all that sympathetic.

'You're gonna help her,' said Kirk.

'I can't, I can't, I can't...'

'You can,' I replied, 'or my man there is gonna do some very, very bad shit to you.'

Carlisle sniffed, pocketed his book, and stood. 'Perhaps,' he told her, 'you should consider a different line of work.'

'I tell them. I always tell them. I can't do it. Can't control it. Bad stuff happens.'

'Break the link,' he said. 'Now.'

'But.. b-b-but...'

Carlisle grabbed her arm and pulled her to her feet, shoving her towards me. 'Do it, or I will find every family member you have, every friend, every pet, and deliver unto each of them a slow, painful death.'

'But it might kill me,' she said, looking in my direction with imploring eyes.

'Do I look like I give a flying fuck?' I replied.

She looked to each of us, then sagged, resigned to her fate. She reached out and took my hand. 'I never wanted this power. Never did. And all your kind have done is push me to use it again and again, no matter what I say.'

'Not interested in your tragic backstory, Madeline,' said Kirk. 'Get on with the helping part.'

Madeline closed her eyes and a single tear escaped and tracked down her cheek. She nodded, opened her eyes again, and a corona of fire erupted above her green hair. Her skin began to glow, and the demons inside of me started to thrash violently. They seemed to know what was happening, and were trying to fight back.

I couldn't look. I closed my eyes and did something I never did. I prayed. Not to a god, but to James. I held on to my love for him and prayed what Madeline was doing would work. I'm not sure how long passed, maybe a minute, maybe an hour, but eventually it became quiet.

A voice. Kirklander. 'Babe? Erin? Are you okay?'

I opened my eyes. Alive. Still alive. Fuck, yeah. I sat up. I could sit up! I could move and feel and all that good stuff. I looked down at my body, my hands touching and prodding all over, searching for any supernatural squatters, but the invaders were gone. No more demons. No impossibly twisted and stretched body. It was as though it had never happened.

I laughed and hugged Kirk, planting kiss after hungry kiss on him. If Carlisle hadn't been standing in the corner I'd have straddled him there and then. Almost did, anyway.

'Thank Christ,' I said, panting like a marathon winner. Rarely had I felt such pure happiness.

'You had me worried there for a minute,' said Kirk, his smile as big as I'd ever seen it.

'It worked? Madeline saved me?'

'Yes,' replied Carlisle.

I felt like I wanted to thank her. Wanted to clear out my bank account and hand her everything I had. Wanted to punch her in both tits for messing me up in the first place. It was a mixed set of emotions for sure.

'Where is she?' I asked.

Carlisle raised an eyebrow and nodded to the floor. I leaned over to see a large pile of ash there.

'Madeline?'

'Yup,' said Kirk.

'What happened?'

'She managed to sever the connection,' said Carlisle, 'only the demons didn't like that too much. She couldn't push them back, so they just hopped into her.'

'They killed her?'

'They most certainly would have done,' replied Carlisle. 'Luckily for you, I was here to kill her first. Eventually one of the demons would have won and emerged from her to feast upon the pair of you. Consider yourself welcome.'

Right. Complicated feelings again, but fuck it, rather her than me, right? Okay, fine, I'll admit I didn't feel all that great about the fact that we'd forced her into helping me, and she'd ended up dead for her troubles, but what was I supposed to do? I didn't have time to wallow in guilt or let it slow me down. Remorse would come later. If there was a later, that is.

I stood, still a little shaky, but alive.

'Weird,' said Kirklander.

'What is?'

'I never knew you before your tattoos.'

I looked down to where he was touching my wrist. I should have seen faded occult symbols etched into my skin. Should have seen them running up my arms, along my collar bones. Instead, I saw skin, My naked skin, bald and unadorned.

My tattoos were completely gone.

20

My ordeal had left me coated in a rancid glaze of stale sweat, and smelling like a fish market, so before I did anything else, I decided, for the sake of my companions, that I'd best take a shower.

Carlisle pointed me down a hallway to a room I could use to get washed up. Clutching a towel, I made my way unsteadily to a small bathroom, where I stripped down and stared at my reflection in the mirror.

I looked weird.

I wasn't all gross and funhouse mirrored like I was with the demons inside me, but still, I looked off. It was the lack of ink. I'd worn those tats since I was a teenager. They were part of me—literally part of me, etched into my skin, over and over again—and now they were gone. I ran my fingertips gently across the top of my chest, tracing shapes that I could no longer see. Shapes that had vanished like sandcastles before the sea.

The ink had made me Uncanny. Given me Insider status. Given me access to a world of magic and monsters and mayhem beyond my imagining. And now... now I was just me again. Erin Gertrude Banks. No magic. No super strength. No powers of regeneration. Just me. And I had no idea who the fuck that was.

I stepped into the bath, toes flinching as they met the tub's chill, white floor. The plumbing moaned like a horror movie ghost as I turned on the hot water and let it beat furiously against my head. I closed my eyes and dragged my fingers through my long, wet hair as the bathroom filled with steam.

So that was that. Well, fuck it, I refused to give up. Call me stubborn if you like—Parker would have, and worse—but I wasn't about to let this setback stop me. Wasn't going to do as L'Merrier insisted and throw in the towel. Wasn't going to ditch The Tenth and forget all about the Red-Eyed Man, about my brother.

I was willing to die to find out the truth. To get revenge. Of course I was. Even with my ink, I'd known that death was a likely outcome. The fact that I was out of ammo didn't change that. This Eternal, this Father, whoever they, he, or it was, they were going to face me, and soon. I could feel the certainty running through me like electricity. The end was coming fast, and I was about to meet it head-on.

———

The Porsche was too small for three people, so we helped ourselves to a roomier vehicle off the street, a four-door coupe with a decent engine and a full tank of petrol. Carlisle instructed Kirklander that he would be the designated driver, before climbing into the rear of the car and stretching out on the back seat. I shrugged at Kirk and got in the passenger seat, the weight of The Tenth heavy in my jacket's inside pocket. Without complaint, Kirklander started the engine, checked his hair in the vanity mirror, and off we went. L'Merrier had told us what The Tenth was for, now it was time to put the thing to use.

I watched Kirklander as he guided us towards Stonehenge, his hand steady on the wheel, shifting gears almost soundlessly. Road lights licked the car bonnet as we sped west, streaking down the motorway at twenty past the limit. Stonehenge was a two hour drive from London, but we'd be there in ninety minutes tops. It was the middle of the night, and traffic was light, so we were dominating the fast lane, making good time. I saw Kirk's eyes twitch to the rearview mirror, which showed Carlisle in the back seat, apparently fast asleep.

'Something on your mind?' I asked.

'More than I usually like,' Kirk replied.

'Spit it out.'

His eyes stayed fixed on the road. 'That thing L'Merrier said about promises of money and power... what do you think he meant by that?'

'I dunno. I guess he meant we might be offered cash and stuff in exchange for handing over the last key.'

'Right,' he said, nodding, thoughtful.

'What?'

'Nothing.'

Oh, Jesus Christ. 'You're not actually considering it?'

'What? Of course not. I was just, you know, wondering.'

'This is about my brother, Kirk. They could offer me all the riches in the world and I wouldn't bat an eyelid.'

'Hey, I was just thinking out loud, that's all. Of course we won't consider anything. It's just interesting to me, that's all.'

We drove in silence for a few minutes after that. Typical Kirklander. Apparently, he hadn't evolved *that* much.

'There was a door,' said Carlisle, his sudden contribution taking us both by surprise.

Kirklander jerked the wheel involuntarily, almost sending us ploughing into the central reservation. 'I thought you were asleep!'

'Oh, I swore off sleep a long time ago,' Carlisle replied.

'A door to what?' I asked.

'To Other London. Its secret streets are woven through the actual city of London, but you can enter and exit the place at many points across the Uncanny Kingdom. At least, you *could*, once upon a time.'

I thought I understood what he was getting at. 'You're saying there used to be a door from Stonehenge that led to Other London?'

'Indeed. Or at least, close enough.'

Other London. The abandoned city that I'd followed my brother to when he was taken by the pig and Scarbury, the Red-Eyed Man.

'Well, that makes sense,' I said. 'If they wanted James for some reason connected to this Eternal bloke, and they needed to get him from Brighton to somewhere else in the country, the doors in and out of Other London would make for a handy shortcut.'

'Quite right.'

I'd spent a lifetime poring over all of this shit. My relentless pursuit of James had bent my family out of shape, turned us against each other, made me into a killer. And now, in the space of a few short months, everything had changed. I'd found the trail that led to the source of it all, and here I was, picking up the breadcrumbs piece by piece, soon to arrive at my journey's end.

So weird.

Weird to be that close to getting what I wanted. And

weird that after years—no, *decades*—of nothing, now I had almost everything. It itched at something in my mind. An itch that I couldn't quite get to.

'Henge-ho,' said Kirklander as we pulled off the A303 and the silhouette of the ancient stone circle hoved into view.

We drove to the site's visitor centre and explained to a security guard that we were there to take some arty, long exposure photos of the henge with star trails in the background (never mind that the light pollution out there would have made that impossible). The guard wasn't entirely convinced, but a well-placed bribe changed his mind, and he lifted the gate, letting us know we had thirty minutes to get our snaps.

Kirk drove us down a dirt path, then pulled to a stop in a coach park and killed the engine. Carlisle stepped out of the back of the car and looked across the whorled expanse of green that Stonehenge sat on, a little way off in the distance. Kirklander and I stayed where we were, sat alone in the front of the car.

'You ready for what happens next?' asked Kirk.

'Of course,' I replied, bristling slightly.

'Good. Because I'm not.'

I softened, holding a hand to Kirk's face. 'I'm starting to have silly thoughts about us two.'

'Yeah, me as well.'

'Silly thoughts like, maybe, if we don't die in the near future, maybe...'

'...maybe we actually try to have one of those grown-up relationship things you see on the telly.'

I smiled and traced the edge of Kirk's lower lip with the tip of my thumb. 'What if one of us falls back into old habits and fucks the other over?' I said.

'Then we can say we tried. As best as we knew how.'

I nodded, then leaned in and kissed him.

It was a nice moment. A moment of hope. The kind of moment that I'd sometimes toy around with when I was alone at night, then dismiss as idiotic. Still, right there and then, about to face off against who knew what, it seemed like something worth holding on to. Sure, maybe it would all go to shit if we actually did try to give it a proper go, but as we kissed, our mouths fitting each other like shapes in the opening minute of a Tetris game, it felt great. Everything was on the table now. Every outcome. Why couldn't we, for once, do the right thing?

Listen to me, getting all soppy. I probably had love hearts for eyes. Jesus, I'm disgusting myself here.

We pulled apart as Carlisle slapped his hand on the car roof. 'When you are both quite ready, children...'

We got out and joined Carlisle.

'So what should we do?' I asked.

'L'Merrier says this is a door. A door with a lock. Let's see if we can discover just where our key fits.'

He strutted off ahead of us, leaving Kirk and I chasing the tail of his purple coat.

Stonehenge isn't as big as you're probably picturing it. Oh, it's impressive for sure, but it's surprisingly small when you get right up in its face. I couldn't deny it was casting a spooky air, though, the black of night cradling the ancient stones as we hopped the rope barrier and stepped into the circle.

'Surely if one of these stones had a keyhole,' said Kirk-lander, scratching his chin stubble, 'someone would have noticed it a long time ago. It's not like these rocks haven't had archaeologists swarming over them for years.'

'He has a point,' I said.

'Yes. A fool with a foolish point. How novel.'

Kirklander rounded on Carlisle, but I stepped in his way. 'Jesus, would you two put your wands away?'

'I've had enough of him,' said Kirk, his eyes boring into Carlisle like two drill bits.

'It's a secret door with a secret lock to a secret monster in a secret realm,' Carlisle shot back. 'It is unlikely that the necessary keyhole would be obvious to any man, woman, or child with a trowel and a thirst for knowledge.'

'Just chill out,' I told Kirk.

He took a breath and softened. 'Fine. Okay.'

'Yes, restrain your lapdog, I'd hate to have to neuter him,' said Carlisle.

'You can shut the fuck up, too,' I said, jabbing a finger in Carlisle's ribs. 'We're on the same side here. Act like it.'

'I am on my own side, alone,' replied Carlisle, brushing the crease from his jacket.

'What an arsehole,' muttered Kirklander, which I really couldn't disagree with.

'Has he told you, yet?' asked Carlisle.

I looked at him, confused. 'Has he told me what?'

'Oh,' Carlisle chuckled. 'Then he has not.'

'Told me what?' I turned to Kirklander. 'Kirk, what is he bollocking on about?'

'What? Nothing,' he replied, obviously lying.

'Tell me.'

'I see the unseen,' said Carlisle. 'At times it is a curse, at others it is just rather amusing. And do you know what I see in him?'

'Shut your mouth,' yelled Kirklander, magic igniting in his fist.

'What do you see?' I demanded.

Carlisle bit the edge of a smile. 'I see nothing.'

'I said, shut up!'

Kirklander moved to unleash his magic in Carlisle's direction. Carlisle rolled up his sleeves. We'd come here as a team, and we'd already degenerated into a squabbling mess. Only, the fight ended before it began. We were no longer alone.

'You have what is ours,' came a whispered voice that made the hairs on the nape of my neck stand to attention.

I turned.

Framed by one of the circle's great, stone arches were two figures.

One was a pig, stood on its hind legs.

The other was Scarbury, his red eyes blazing like two angry suns.

21

Three against two seems like pretty good odds, right? Especially when one of the enemies you're facing off against is, you know, a pig. Of course, this wasn't your average pig. Even without his magic, it was clear this specimen wasn't your ordinary farmyard porker. Unless you often find yourself crossing paths with pigs that stand up like a person, talk in English, and wear natty little outfits. So yeah, there were three of us and two of them, but I didn't feel like the odds were particularly in our favour, especially as I'd arrived to the party without a sniff of magic on me.

'The Tenth,' said Scarbury, reaching out a hand blacker than the surrounding night, 'give it to me.'

'You want the moon on a stick, you do,' I replied.

'You have no choice but to part with it,' said Scarbury, 'none of us do. This has all been written. What has come before, and what will happen again.'

'Not a big reader,' I said. 'Maybe you can give me the edited highlights.'

Scarbury's eyes blazed brighter, just for a second.

'Hello, my name is Carlisle. I believe you robbed a portion of my memory.'

The pig grunted and sniggered.

'I really hate that little fucker,' Kirklander whispered in my ear.

'The Tenth,' said Scarbury. 'You found it and brought it here, just as we knew you would.'

'Look, enough of all the fucking, "It is foretold", nonsense, okay? Tell me why you took my brother before we hammer the two of you into the ground.'

Scarbury didn't answer, didn't even move.

'Fine, if you and Piglet wanna keep things close to your chest, how about I destroy The Tenth and see where that leaves you?'

'You cannot.'

'I bloody well can.'

'No. The Tenth cannot be destroyed, it is indestructible.'

'Fine. No problem. I'll just make it my life's work to keep it from you then, you cherry-eyed fuck. I'll run, and I'll keep on running. You'll never get your hands on it. I'll sleep with it under my pillow. I'll keep it on me every single day.'

'Will you now?' he scoffed, the pig grunting at his side, the two of them obviously finding the whole thing incredibly funny for some reason.

'Yeah, I'll keep your precious key nice and safe. Safe from you and your curly-tailed fuck buddy.'

Scarbury's mouth formed a cruel smile. 'If that is so, you are not doing a very good job of it.'

'What? What are you...?'

That's when I noticed something odd. My jacket felt light. I touched the leather over where the pocket was and found it empty.

'Oh dear,' said Scarbury.

A spike of anger rose inside of me. I'd been robbed. Someone had lifted The Tenth from me. I turned to Kirklander, snarling.

'What did you do?'

He'd sold me out. All that talk of wealth and power on the way here, I should have known. He hadn't changed at all, he was still just looking out for himself. How could I have fallen for it again? How could I have been so fucking stupid? There were so many red flags you could have seen them from outer space.

'What?' said Kirklander, taking a step back as though the look on my face had physically pushed him away.

'It's all bullshit, isn't it? It always is with you. I give you chance after chance, but you never miss an opportunity to stab me in the back.'

'What are you talking about?'

'Don't lie to me. Don't you lie to me any more!'

I heard a polite cough from behind. 'Perhaps I could interject,' said Carlisle.

I turned to him and saw he was holding The Tenth.

'You?'

'I did warn you that I was a thief when we first met, assassin. A thief, a criminal, and more besides.'

The pig threw his head back, grunting and wheezing, whisking his fat blue tongue around his lips.

'This has all been written,' said Scarbury.

I felt as though the ground had been pulled out from under me. I was rolling down a hill, out of control, barrelling blindly into oncoming traffic. 'What are you doing?' I quavered.

'Playing my hand,' replied Carlisle.

'Give it back,' said Kirk, his voice cold as steel.

'I'm afraid not.'

'We're in this together,' I said. 'They did this to you, too. Took your memories.'

Carlisle frowned, then shrugged. 'True, I did find that extremely irksome. I intended to have more than a few cross words with these gentlemen, but then having heard what L'Merrier had to say... well, the promise of power and riches quickly soothed any grievances I'd been holding on to.'

When the Long Man showed me the fractured piece of memory I'd lost, the one revealing Carlisle, I'd worried. I'd been suspicious of the man from the first time I met him, had my guard up right from the off. I knew he couldn't be trusted, but I'd trusted him anyway. A bit of a running theme with me, eh? And now, as we reached the end of the road, another man had decided his greed outweighed my pain.

'Give it back or I'll take it from you.'

Carlisle smiled. 'Oh, I think not.'

Scarbury turned to Carlisle. 'The Tenth. Give it to me.'

A broken record, this guy.

Kirklander stepped towards Carlisle. 'You're handing that over to us or I'm going to magic your head into your small intestine.'

Carlisle clicked his fingers. The ground beneath our feet erupted as though a landmine had been triggered, sending Kirk and me sprawling to the dirt.

'Threats are only threatening if you have the ability to back them up, pretty boy.'

'Eat shit!' said Kirk, punching out a fist and sending a wave of intertwining ribbons of magic into Carlisle's chest.

The blast lifted the wizard off his feet and sent him hurtling back like a fish yanked on an angler's line.

'How do you like that, dickless?' Kirklander yelled as we got to our feet, mud tumbling from our clothes.

Carlisle landed on his feet, stable as a table, then began running straight towards us, his long coat billowing behind him like a cape, its lining flashing with starlight.

'Right then,' said Kirk.

'No.' I tried to grab him, to pull him back, but he was too fast for me. If I'd had my tattoos—my enhanced speed and strength—I might have managed to reach out and snatch him back in time, but I didn't. 'Kirk, stop!'

It was no use. All I could do was watch. Watch as Kirklander ran headlong at the rapidly advancing Carlisle. Magic swarmed around him, building in intensity, ready to be unleashed, ready to take Carlisle's head off. Only, he never got the chance. Carlisle was too good, too quick, too strong. He clapped his hands together and created a strange pulse that made the air ripple. Kirk was scooped off his feet and sent spinning away like an out of control Catherine Wheel. On a lucky day, he'd have landed in a limp heap on the grass and come up for more. This wasn't one of those days.

Kirklander struck one of the henge's stone pillars and made a sound like an ice cube cracking in water, only a hundred times the volume. His body crumpled, then down to the dirt he dropped, leaving a red stain on the stone behind him. I didn't need my tattoos to move fast then, I was at Kirk's side in a heartbeat.

'Kirk? Kirk? Kirk, listen to me. Can you hear me? Please.'

Blood was pouring from his skull, rushing out like the yolk from a broken egg.

'Please, Kirk. Please don't leave me.'

I became aware of a figure standing over me. I looked up to see Carlisle, his expression unreadable. 'Now that is bad luck,' he said.

I had a knife in my pocket. I wanted to take it out.

Wanted to slide it between Carlisle's ribs and drive it into his heart. But I couldn't stand. Could barely move.

'No hard feelings, I hope,' said Carlisle, then spun on his heel to face the pig and Scarbury.

He tossed The Tenth from one hand to the other as he approached his new companions. The view through one of the stone arches warped and rippled, then the three of them stepped beneath it, heading into the portal. Scarbury and the pig vanished through the gateway immediately, disappearing with a sound like a plughole emptying. Carlisle paused and took one last look over his shoulder, then he bowed his head to me slightly, stepped through the arch, and blinked from existence.

22

I t's funny, you only really know how strongly you feel for someone when they're suddenly not there any more.

Maybe you split up. Maybe they died. But once they're out of the picture, that's when it really hits. That horrible ache of lost love. That thing you questioned over and over, wondering if it was even real, yet the moment they're gone, that's when all uncertainty melts away. When it becomes obvious. So obvious that you wonder how you could ever have doubted it.

I leaned Kirklander back against the standing stone that had killed him, his body limp and heavy in my arms. Things had really gone to shit fast. How had this happened? I thought I'd be the one who wound up dead, not Kirk. I'd pulled him into this mess. This was my fault. He'd put his life on the line for me, and that's exactly what it had cost him. Why had he chosen this mission not to flake on me? Couldn't he have bailed out like he always did? Why did he have to go and grow a conscience this time? I'd wanted him to change, wanted us both to change, and look where it had got us.

It was all over. Kirklander was dead, my connection to magic dead. One half of my back-up had suffered a lethal blow, the other had double-crossed me. What was I supposed to do from here? I couldn't carry on alone. I'd had my chance at revenge and lost it. Yeah, things had really gone to shit.

A rumble...

I felt it in the ground I was slumped upon. A slight trembling. A low sound on the edge of my perception. What was that? An earthquake?

A flash of red light blinded me, accompanied by a sound like a metal gong being struck. I rubbed at my eyes and blinked over and over until my vision cleared. A large figure had joined me.

'Gerald?'

Gerald was a giant of a man, dressed in a fine, expensive suit. I'd worked with him several times before. Well, I'd worked for his master, the demonic Long Man, a creature who lived in a realm that could only be accessed through Gerald.

'Hello, Ms Banks,' he said in his flat, monosyllabic voice.

'How did you... how are you here?'

'When it is time, I arrive. In an instant, I am there. It is my gift. One of my gifts.'

I shook my head as if trying to dislodge something. I couldn't piece together what was happening. Shock, horror, loss, all swarmed like bees inside of me. 'Time for what?'

'A deal was made. Now it is time to collect.'

Gerald kneeled down, opened his jacket, and unbuttoned his shirt.

And then things began to slot into place. The Long Man

dealt in promises. Dealt in souls. If you could get his ear, you could offer your eternal spirit in return for something that you wanted. Then, when it came time to collect, Gerald would appear and the debt would be paid.

'But... he can't have...'

I wanted to ask more questions, but I was out of time.

Gerald threw his head back as a giant, clawed hand burst from his torso. It reached out and out and wrapped its fingers around Kirklander's corpse, plucking him from the ground as if he were a child's toy.

'No!' I stumbled back in shock as the Long Man's hand yanked Kirklander back towards Gerald. *Inside* of Gerald.

'Don't you dare!'

Panic overwhelmed me, but one thing shone bright and clear through the confusion. I couldn't let Kirklander go. If I waited, that would be it. He'd be gone, and gone for good. Without thinking it through, I pushed myself to my feet and ran towards the now kneeling Gerald. Ran towards his gaping, split-open torso. A torso that was already beginning to fuse together, closing the door to the Long Man's realm.

A metre out, I jumped. Arms outstretched, I dove into Gerald and landed in a heap on the barren, rocky surface of the Long Man's realm. I got to my feet, a sharp wind pulling at my hair.

'Long Man,' I screamed, the wind so wild that my words sounded muffled in my ears.

The Black Cathedral stood before me fashioned from smooth, jet black blocks of stone, its giant spire snapped and fallen, lying beside it like a shattered spine. I ran over the loose stones that littered the barren ground and pushed my way inside the building.

'Long Man, I wanna see you,' I yelled, my voice bouncing around the stone innards of the vaulted building.

'You, is it?' said the Old Woman with her eyes sewn shut.

'Stay out of this, you old bag. I'm busy.'

'Yes, I knows it. Busy and wicked and sad. Paying for your sins.'

'Oh, fuck off,' I said and strode past her towards the altar.

'Charming,' muttered the Old Woman, before limping off towards the exit.

'Long Man, now!'

The Black Cathedral rippled around me as though someone had dropped a stone into the waters of a calm lake. Once it had settled again, I was no longer in the building. I was stood outside in a forest, the Long Man's Forest of Souls. All around me, gnarled trees reached up into the sky like hands bursting from the grave. Each tree was once a person, or the soul of a person, at least. The Long Man took the souls of his debtors and planted them, and each of those souls would mutate into a tree. A tree that would scream in agony every time the moon hung high.

The Long Man was stood waiting for me, a sinister leer on his elongated skull. Kirklander's corpse lay crumpled at his cloven feet, his soul ready to be planted.

'Erin Banks. I did not request your presence.'

'I have a habit of showing up where I'm not wanted.'

'His soul is mine.'

'Cool, cool. One question: what the fuck is going on?'

The Long Man crouched down on his haunches. 'He desired. He wanted. All who find me do.'

'What did he want?'

And then it hit me. Of course. How else had Kirklander managed to transform into a master of the mystical arts except by selling his soul to the devil? He'd been trying to tell me and chickening out ever since I turned up at his door, out of my mind, during the whole Liyta business.

Idiot.

Idiot!

'He wouldn't...'

'He did. Most who do never believe they would agree to such a thing. Not until the words are leaving their mouths and the deal is done.'

The Long Man gestured to a hole in the soil, ready to accept Kirklander's soul.

'Wait. Wait just wait a second. There must be something we can do.'

'There is. I am doing it. He got what he wanted and then he died. The terms of the contract are clear, so I collect.'

My heart was beating so fast that I worried the demon would soon find not one but two corpses littering his forest.

'You can bring him back.'

The Long Man tilted his head to one side and inspected me with an unfathomable gaze.

'I know you can. I've been working with you for months now, you think I haven't researched this shit? I know it's in your power to restore someone whose soul you own, at least if you do it within a half hour of their death.'

The Long Man said nothing.

'It's true. It is true, isn't it?'

A pause, then the Long Man nodded his huge, horned head.

'Then do it. Bring Kirklander back to life.'

Again, the Long Man said nothing.

'Do it. Do it now!'

He reached down and lifted Kirk's body, studying it. 'Why would I?'

'Because... because I said so, that's why.'

'You desire him?'

'Up yours.'

The Long Man stared at me, and an icy chill crept up my spine.

'Fine. I love the dumb fuck, so what?'

'He agreed to my terms. He received what he desired. He died. The contract is complete. His soul is mine.'

The Long Man scooped Kirklander's body up in his massive claws and carried him to the soul hole.

'Fuck. Fuck!' I paced back and forth, fists clenching and unclenching. 'Okay. Okay. New deal.'

'He has no voice to bargain with. His soul is already mine.'

As the idea formed inside of me, I knew it was stupid. Worse than stupid. Was this what caring did to a person? Was this what love forced you to do?

'What about... what about *two* souls?'

The Long Man lowered Kirklander's body to the ground and leaned closer to me.

'Go on.'

'You won't relinquish ownership of his soul, right?'

He shook his head.

'Then just wait on collecting. Give him a second chance to live before he's yours. And in return...' I took a breath, considered stopping, called myself a few colourful names, then got on with it, 'and in return you can have my soul, too.'

He looked at Kirk's body, then back to me. 'This is... interesting.'

'Yeah, I thought it would be up your alley.'

Something that might have been a smile flashed across the Long Man's skull face. 'Continue.'

'You bring him back to life, now, and the two of us leave

here, live our lives—which are likely to be pretty fucking short anyway—and in return you can add my soul to your list. I'll even work for you. Be your emissary. Whenever you want, I'll do it for free.'

I shut my mouth before I started offering up anything else. I was so eager for him to agree that I think I'd have promised him just about anything.

The demon stroked his long chin.

'Well?' I cried. 'Say something, you big bastard.'

'Are you sure?'

I looked at Kirklander's corpse and didn't even pause to question myself. 'Yeah,' I replied. 'I'm sure.'

'You are stupid.'

'It's been said before.'

'Your link to the Uncanny is severed. Without your tattoos, you no longer have access to magic. Your offer to work for me is useless if you are merely human.'

Fuck.

'Okay, I'll work out the kinks. I met a woman with a magic axe a while back, maybe I rob the bitch and get myself tooled up.'

The Long Man reached out towards me.

'Whoa there, what are you...?'

'Shh...'

The tip of one great claw touched my forehead and the world exploded. My body felt like it was on fire, like daggers heated over a forge were being stuck in me, over and over, and I couldn't move, couldn't squirm out of the way, couldn't even scream. Then as quickly as the torture began, it ended.

I stumbled back, knees unhinging. 'What the fuck? What did you do to me?'

But the demon didn't have to answer. I felt it. I looked down at my arms. Peeking out from the cuffs of my jacket were shapes, occult symbols tattooed on my skin. A smile spread across my face as I pushed my sleeves up and felt the ink throb.

'Holy shit!'

My tattoos. My connection to magic. I was hooked up to the mains again.

I pulled magic into me, a reflex, I barely had to think about it. My new tattoos glowed as power soaked into them, and I immediately felt like I'd grown a foot in height. The molecules that made up my body seemed to tremble and pulsate, vibrating so fast that I felt like I could phase through brick walls. I was back. I was back, baby!

Only... it felt a little different.

Make that *a lot* different.

It wasn't like with Madeline's botched job. No, this wasn't a mistake, it just felt like the magic that was flooding into me this time was stronger. Older. Darker.

'You are now connected to the magic of my realm,' said the Long Man.

'But that's... dark magic,' I gasped, watching as electricity arced between my tattoos, crackling with forbidden energy.

He nodded. 'It might take some time to... grow comfortable with.'

The magic I'd grown used to, the supernatural energy given off by all living things, felt warm. But this? It felt cold. It felt like ice cubes rubbing along my bones.

'Is it dangerous?' I asked.

The Long Man smiled.

I could feel it, this new magic, ancient and angry and desperate to destroy. Magic let you do things, let you create. Yes, it could be used as a weapon, but that was a byproduct, a perversion of its true function. But this magic... this magic only had one thing on its mind. Oh yeah, it was dangerous all right.

'This new power of yours will not die,' said the Long Man. 'Your connection to it is permanent.'

'Wait, you're telling me I never have to sit in a tattoo chair again?'

The demon shook his head.

That was a definite bonus. Sure, I'd promised my soul to a demon, but this softened the stupidity of that decision considerably, even if the magic I felt coursing through my veins scared the hell out of me.

'What about Kirklander?' I asked.

'Remove him from my realm. When you exit, he will live.'

I couldn't help but smile. 'Thanks. Thank you.'

'You are mine now,' the Long Man intoned gravely.

I tried to frown but the smile refused to budge.

'You will work for me. Both of you. And one day, in the blink of an eye as far as eternity is concerned, I will claim what is mine and you will stand forever in this forest.'

'Cheery thought.'

'It is done.'

The air rippled and I was no longer in the forest. I was back in front of the Black Cathedral, Kirk at my feet, the Long Man gone.

'Well, this might be the dumbest thing you've ever done, Erin,' I told myself.

I crouched and picked up Kirklander's dead weight. It should have been difficult, but with my cold tattoos burning electric blue, I might as well have been hoisting a baby boy.

I looked at the Black Cathedral, then turned and headed towards the exit of the Long Man's realm.

23

I crawled through the exit portal and found myself back at Stonehenge. I emerged in the centre of the stone circle, the large blocks of grey rock looming over me, the scene as quiet as a crypt.

Reaching back into the portal, I grabbed hold of Kirklander's arm and dragged him out through the open wound in Gerald's belly. Once he was clear, Gerald stood, his open torso knitting back together. He calmly buttoned his shirt and jacket.

'What now?' I asked, looking down at Kirklander, who laid there unmoving, pale and blue-lipped.

No response.

I looked up to find Gerald gone. I turned sharply in surprise, scanning left and right, but he was nowhere to be seen. The Long Man's emissary had vanished as suddenly as he had arrived.

'Hey!' I shouted. 'What happens now? He's dead. He's still dead!'

No sooner had the words left my mouth than Kirklander's eyes snapped open, wide and terrified. He spasmed, arching his body, desperately drawing air into his lungs.

'Kirk!'

He rolled onto his side and vomited, coughing and trembling. I dropped to my knees beside him, hands gripping his shoulders like a bird of prey.

'It's okay. You're okay. Just breathe.'

It took a minute or two before all the lights were back on and he could get himself under control.

'What... the fuck...?' he wheezed, his voice as rough as a badger's arse.

'You just came back from the dead. Give it a minute.'

His eyes met mine, wild. 'I did what?'

'Remember Carlisle?'

He sat up fast, almost threw up again, swallowed it down, then swore.

'Yeah. You smacked your head on one of the stones. Hard. Hard enough to kill you.'

I pointed at the splotch of red on the column he'd collided with. He reached a hand to his head and felt for a wound. His coiffure was matted with blood, but the damage he'd suffered was gone. I parted his hair and examined him closer under the moonlight. His cracked skull was fused, good as new.

'I... I died?' he stammered.

'Yup.'

'Holy fuck.'

'Yup.'

He pressed a hand to his chest as if to check that his soul was still where it should be.

'How? How am I...?'

'First of all, you have no idea how pissed off I am at you.'

'I don't understand any of this—'

'Second, you're alive because I'm a fucking idiot.' I leaned forward and pressed my lips against his.

He pulled away suddenly. 'Wait. I don't understand. If I died, how come I'm not dead? Isn't that the way these things usually go?'

'The reason you're not dead is because I had a word with the Long Man.'

Kirk's eyes narrowed. 'What did you do?'

'I saved you.'

'What did you do?' he repeated, louder this time, his fingertips digging into my forearm.

'I made a deal, okay? Since you were dumb enough to sell your soul, the only way to help you was to do something just as stupid.'

Kirklander stood and whirled away from me, furious. 'I can't believe you did that.'

'It was the only way.'

'Fuck. Fuck!'

'Yeah, I fully agree.'

He walked back to me and knelt down so that we were face-to-face again. 'So now?'

'Now we both owe the Long Man a soul.'

'And you did that for me?'

I frowned. Nodded.

'Why?'

'You know why.'

His eyes searched mine for a second, then he saw it. Saw the reason I did what I did. Our lips met again, our bodies pressed together, but this was more than lust. This was something beyond that, something far beyond.

When we finally parted, Kirklander laughed and shook his head. 'You're a lunatic, you know that?'

'I must be.'

I stood and turned to the stone arch that Carlisle had disappeared through along with Scarbury and the pig. The air between it still rippled ever so slightly. The doorway was still open. That was good. Was that good? Why was it still open? Maybe they wanted me to follow. Which would mean I shouldn't.

I already knew I would.

'Hey, your tats are back,' said Kirk, taking my wrist and turning my arm over to inspect my new ink.

'Another part of the deal.' I shivered slightly and the tattoos flared and sent a chill through my body. That was going to take some getting used to.

'We are both so fucked, aren't we?'

'At some point, absolutely. But until then, we keep going. And who knows, maybe somewhere in between we'll figure a way out of this mess.'

Kirklander didn't look too convinced. 'So what now?' he asked, his hand slipping into mine.

'Now we go after them. I'm not done yet. Not until I get answers. Not until someone pays. You with me?'

Kirk flashed me the kind of smile that had led to me losing my clothes too many times to count. 'Always, babe.'

'Good.'

I walked forward, Kirk at my side, and we stepped through the arch together.

At first, everything was a pure, blinding white. Then the white dimmed and turned black. And then we were somewhere else.

A biting cold numbed my face and sent my teeth chattering. At first, I thought the sudden chill was the fault of my new ink, but it had nothing to do with that. The reason I was cold was because wherever we were, the temperature had dropped by a good ten degrees.

'Christ, it's cold as the witch's tit out here,' said Kirk, shivering, 'and I would know. Did I ever tell you about my brief affair with Maria, the head witch of the Cardiff Coven?'

I ignored Kirk as I turned in a circle, taking in our surroundings. We were in a tunnel bored through solid rock. The walls were damp, with flaming torches bolted to them that bathed the tunnel in a flickering orange light.

'We're underground,' I said.

'Under Stonehenge, do you think?'

'Makes sense,' I replied. 'I wonder how far down this is?'

Stonehenge was a lock, that's what L'Merrier had said. But there had been no evidence of a keyhole above ground. If Carlisle and the others had been transported way down here, under Stonehenge, it stood to reason that there was a hole that The Tenth could slot into beneath the above-ground bit.

I took a look in both directions. 'Which way?'

'I say we go that way,' replied Kirklander, pointing in the direction I was facing.

'Why?'

'Because of them,' he said, now pointing behind me. I turned to see people emerging from the dark.

'Oh.'

There were two of them at first, but within seconds there were six, eleven, twenty. More and more people crowding in behind, silently watching us. They were dressed in normal clothes, but there was one strange thing about them: they all wore masks. The masks had been carved from wood, simple ovals with two small, dark holes for eyes.

'Is it just me, or is this seriously creepy?' asked Kirklander.

'It's not just you.'

We began to retreat from the crowd of mask-wearing strangers. As we did this, they suddenly began to move as one, surging, screaming down the tunnel towards us.

'Shit on a brick,' yelled Kirk, punching out, magic rushing from his hands and striking the first row of attackers.

The vanguard were knocked down by a sheet of purple fire and set aflame, but the wave behind them didn't let up. They scrambled over the fallen, clawing over their blazing bodies, not caring for their own lives. Kirk punched out again and again, knocking down row after row of them, but still they came.

'Maybe we should do a bit of running?' I suggested.

'Great idea.'

We turned and legged it from the rapidly advancing swarm. The tunnel forked in two, but we didn't get to choose one way or the other. The fork to the left had more people running down it towards us, so we went right. The same thing happened a second time, a third.

'Why do I feel like cattle being herded towards the slaughterhouse?' asked Kirklander.

'Look,' I said, pointing ahead to where the pig stood, waving at us.

'After the little fucker.'

The pig turned and ran around a corner, disappearing out of view. By the time we rounded the bend, he was gone, skipping through an open metal door. We stumbled through after him and slammed the door shut behind us. Kirk pressed his palms to the metal and fused it shut just as a deafening welter of fists arrived, pummelling the other side of the door, desperate to get through and tear us to pieces.

'That was...' Kirklander fell silent as he swivelled his head to look past me. 'Oh, shit.'

I turned to take in the room we'd locked ourselves into. It was a simple, stone-walled room, with only one way in or out, and the pig was nowhere to be seen. In the centre of the room, jutting down from the ceiling, was what looked like one of the stones that made up the henge above. There was a gap of about seven feet, then directly under that, a second henge stone pushed its way up out of the ground. Light shone between the stones, a pure white light. But it was what floated between these two monolithic stones, suspended in the column of light, that really caught the eye.

A man.

He was naked, his eyes closed, his hair short and dark. He looked to be in his early twenties.

I took a step forward and the sound of fists against the metal door behind us seemed to fade away.

I knew who the man was.

I didn't know how—it made no sense that I could be so certain—but I was sure.

Sure despite the fact that the last time I'd seen him he'd been a baby.

My baby brother.

'James?'

24

Kirklander was saying something, but I couldn't hear him.

I reached out to touch my brother, to pull him down, but the column of light he was suspended inside of wouldn't let me in.

All that time. All those years. And there he was.

Part of me had hoped James was still alive—of course it had—but I'd never counted on that part being right. He would be dead. It went without saying. What possible reason could there be for him still being around? Though I might have entertained fantasies of finding James alive and rescuing him, I knew the idea of seeing him again was nonsense. I always knew that. I was happy to let the delusions warm me at night, but the cold light of day always chased that hope away.

'Erin!'

He'd be dead. Long dead. For years and years and years. I wouldn't find him alive, wouldn't find him grown-up, wouldn't find him at all. Not a trace of him. I knew all I could really do was find the truth, find the why, and then make the people who took him pay. Get revenge, bloody, painful, revenge for James. For my family. For me.

He was dead.

Would be dead.

Of course he would be.

And yet there I was, standing in front of a fully-grown man that I knew with every fibre of my being was my brother.

They didn't kill him. They'd let him grow. They'd kept him preserved.

Why?

Hands turned me around.

Kirk looking at me, his face etched with worry. 'Erin, can you hear me?'

I blinked and shook my head, the sound of fists clamouring to knock down the door coming back to me loud and clear.

'It's him, Kirk.'

'Are you sure?'

I nodded. It felt like a dream. Maybe it was a dream. Maybe I was lying paralysed on Carlisle's bed, infected with bad magic, hallucinating wildly, and all this was just some Jacob's Ladder scenario. Or was I in the Long Man's realm still? Had he pretended to give me what I wanted, but really I was curled up in his forest of souls? Was the demon digging a fresh hole next to the one he'd scooped out for Kirklander, ready to plant our souls next to each other for all eternity?

'Holy shit,' said Kirklander, slapping me on the back. 'Well, that's good, right? Isn't that good?'

'Yeah. Yeah, I think so. I mean, yes. It is. It's great.'

I was babbling, grabbing at words like a barbecue skewer picking up the last scraps of a meat buffet. My mind was in free fall. I needed to get my shit together. I'd found my brother and he needed my help.

I grimaced, gritted my teeth, and shook myself out of my stupor. The tattoos on my arms burned blue, burned cold, and I could feel my body flooding with power.

With something else, too.

It was wild magic the Long Man had given me. The power raging inside me was like a rabid dog, straining at its leash, desperate to break free. It wanted nothing more than for me to loosen my grip and let it go on a rampage. It wanted to bare its teeth and draw blood.

I controlled my breathing and the untamed feeling began to dial back a little. My hands shook uncontrollably. This new magic was more than I'd ever handled before. Maybe it was too much for me. Maybe using it would tear me apart.

I turned back to my brother. Kirk was kneeling beside the stone that rose up from beneath James' floating body.

'Check this out,' he said.

I joined him to see a small, thin stone protruding from a hole in the stone.

'The Tenth?' I said.

'Maybe, or one of the other nine. Look,' he replied, circling the floor stone, 'they're all here, slotted into this larger one. This must be the keyhole, hidden way down here, out of sight.'

As we walked around to the back of the floor stone, we found where The Tenth was slotted. We knew that was the stone we'd snatched from Chad and brought to Stonehenge, mainly because it was still in Carlisle's hand.

He was laid out on the floor, eyes wide and bulging. His fist was wrapped around The Tenth, which he'd slotted into place before winding up on the ground somehow.

'Is he dead?' asked Kirklander. 'Please say yes, I could use a bit of good news.'

I crouched by Carlisle's side and tentatively reached out to touch his neck. 'He's still breathing, just about.'

'Maybe I should do something about that,' Kirk suggested.

I heard a sharp creak of metal behind us.

'They're gonna get through,' said Kirk. 'Those fuckers are gonna break the door down. It was nice of you to bring me back to life, Erin, but it looks like you bought me another twenty minutes at best.'

Carlisle was trembling slightly.

I grabbed hold of him. 'Can you hear me you double-crossing bastard? What happened?'

He didn't move. Whatever had happened to him, he wasn't in the room any more.

The door hinges wrenched away from the wall slightly.

'Shit,' said Kirklander, rubbing his hands together and forming ribbons of intertwining magic. 'Don't worry, I'll create a circle of protection.'

I nodded, but I wasn't really listening. Now I was next to Carlisle, things had started to slide away again. I found myself pulling Carlisle's hand free of The Tenth and letting his arm flop to the ground.

I turned to the floor stone with all of the ten keys inserted around it. A key, in a lock, ready to turn.

I moved towards it.

It was weird. It was like I was playing a part. Performing a role. Responding to stage directions.

'You have no choice. This has all been written.' That's what Scarbury had told me. Maybe he was right.

The door came down like a drawbridge, landing with an almighty crash. Kirklander spun on the spot, forming a protective ward around us. A ward that no one would be able to break. For a while. I wondered how long.

My hand reached out towards The Tenth. What was I going to do? Maybe I was going to pull it out. Scarbury said it couldn't be destroyed, but maybe he was bluffing. It was just stone, right? Stone could be crushed. Broken down. Was that what I was going to do?

'Tough luck, fuck-nuggets,' Kirklander cried as the swarm of masked lunatics flooded into the room, surrounding us, pressing up against the invisible barrier he'd conjured.

Scarbury and the pig were with them. My fingers were almost touching The Tenth now. Why was I moving so slowly? Did I know this was wrong? The magic in my tattoos writhed, wanting to escape, begging to be unleashed.

'We're gonna destroy your lock, you bunch of weirdos!' screamed Kirklander.

The crowd took off their wooden masks. Beneath, were ordinary faces. Smiling faces.

'This is how it was written,' said Scarbury.

The pig threw back his head and laughed as the crowd began to clap and cheer.

'Erin, are you okay?' asked Kirklander.

My fingertips touched The Tenth.

As I wrapped my fingers around it, I looked up at James. At my brother. His eyes were open. He was looking down at me.

He was smiling.

25

I wasn't where I was.

Maybe it had all been a dream after all.

No.

No, no, no.

It hadn't been a dream.

But I wasn't where I was.

I'd been holding The Tenth, people had been clapping, cheering, laughing. Kirklander had been swearing.

Then nothing.

Then something.

I had my eyes shut.

I wasn't in the room below Stonehenge any more, I knew that. I'd been taken somewhere. By who?

I didn't like the look on my brother's face. That smile as he'd looked down at me. It had been...

I was searching for the right word.

Malevolent. That was it. He'd looked malevolent.

What had they done to my brother?

I opened my eyes.

I wasn't where I was.

I was in space.

Weird.

I was floating through the infinite black of the universe, passing stars and planets and swirling clouds of radiant dust. It was probably beautiful, but it's difficult to appreciate cosmic wonder in that sort of situation.

How did I get in space? And more to the point, how come I wasn't dead? I was breathing. I shouldn't have been able to breathe, not in space. Or was I breathing? I couldn't really tell.

Okay, don't panic, you've been in stranger situations than this.

'No you haven't, what the fuck are you talking about?' I said, chiding myself. Wait, not only shouldn't I be able to breathe in space, I shouldn't be able to hear myself. If the movie *Alien* had taught me anything, it was that in space, no one could hear you scream.

I screamed.

Yup. I could *definitely* hear myself.

Also, I should be freezing. No, way colder than freezing. But I felt...

....Well, I wasn't sure. Wasn't sure how I felt. Wasn't sure of anything.

But at least I wasn't dead.

Unless I was. Maybe I was in the Long Man's realm. A tree in his Forest of Souls.

I wondered where Kirklander was. Wondered if he was okay.

I'd found my brother. He was alive, but I didn't like the look in his eyes.

Shit.

There was something in the dark. Something just as

dark. Something enormous, following me. Best not to think about that. Look the other way, Erin.

Scarbury had said reality was working to a script. That it had all been written. Back under Stonehenge, I'd felt like I'd locked into that story for a moment. That I was no longer in control. That I was just following instructions that someone else had jotted down for me. I didn't like that. Didn't like that at all. I decided what I did and how I acted. Nobody else.

Bollocks. I was gonna have to give the thing following me a closer look, soon.

I hadn't liked the look in my brother's eyes.

My tattoos. I tried to call to them. Tried to pull magic into myself: the cold, hungry, wild magic that I now had access to. Nothing happened. There was nothing there. It was like before the Long Man had given it to me. I was just me in that place. In space. Just me, no magic, floating through the cosmos, impossibly alive.

The thing was making its move. Like a giant whale, it had kicked its great tail and began its journey towards me. I tried to move, tried to swish my arms like I could paddle away. Swim through the black as though it really were a whale chasing me, and we weren't in outer space, we were in the ocean. Not only did it not work, but I couldn't move my arms a fucking inch. Did I even have arms any more? I couldn't feel them. I couldn't feel anything.

A noise.

Clapping?

A room full of people, shouting and cheering.

'Erin!'

'Where are you, Kirk?'

I turned my head. I think I did. If I had a head, it turned, and I saw the beast in the black surging towards me. It opened a single eye as large as a moon, and I think I started to scream again.

In space, Erin Banks can hear you scream.

The beast opened its mouth and swallowed me whole.

'Where are you, Kirk?'

And then...

...

'Erin?'

...

...

...

My eyes were closed again.

I opened them.

It was night-time and I was laid out on a bed of grass. I could feel it beneath me, thousands of cold, dewy blades lying flat beneath my back. I wiggled my fingers, enjoying the texture, the temperature.

I could feel again!

I sat up. I was on the green behind the council estate I lived in as a kid. The estate I'd lived in when James was taken.

'I'm here to tell you,' said a voice, low and gravelly.

'Hey, piggy,' I said. The pig was stood beside me, looking up at the window of James' room.

I stood and turned to find James hanging in the air, surrounded by a ball of red magic.

'I was just in space,' I told the pig.

He nodded and snorted. 'I tell you now.'

'Why?'

He shrugged. 'Because this is how it written. This how I read it. We meet here and we talk and I tell.'

I shrugged, happy to have a body and not be in space being swallowed by a giant, well, whatever-the-fuck.

'I'm listening.'

'Follow, follow,' the pig insisted, beckoning me on with one of his fore-trotters as he walked away, James in his cradle of magic, keeping pace above.

I looked back at my old home, and nodded. 'I guess I've got nothing else on.'

I caught up and walked alongside him, through my old neighbourhood, passing a burned out car sat on four concrete blocks.

'The Eternal. Father. You free him.'

'Nope,' I replied. 'Don't think I do.'

'Do. Will. Both. I read it.'

I thought about breaking the pig's neck, but decided that might be considered rude. In any case, I figured I should at least hold off until he'd spilled everything he knew.

'Go on.'

'A great service, we do. Both do. Both important. You are loved.'

'Aw, you're making me all warm and fuzzy inside, Snuffles.'

'I am important. You important. Brother important. I find. I guide. He vessel. You key.'

He stopped at the end of an alleyway and clapped his trotters together. A small door appeared. He opened it and we stepped through. Through to Other London.

'This place was a shortcut from Brighton to Stonehenge,' I said.

The pig nodded. 'All written. Story of the Endless and his return. The vessel. The key.'

'What does that mean? The key, the vessel?'

'You. And him. Prophecy as written.'

'What's prophecy? Just that this Endless Father bloke is about to return?'

'Return. And how return. Two children, related children, each born on particular dates, at particular times. All known. All written. Had to wait. Had to search. I found you both. Knew I would. Was written. And so I did.'

People walked by us like afterimages. Like ghosts. Going about their lives, lives that had happened decades before, in the cobbled, narrow streets of Other London. Tall, thin, Victorian buildings leaning down to watch us as we passed by.

'I'm part of the prophecy?'

'Part. Important. Knew you would bring final key. Had to be you. We could not collect. We knew where, but not how written. Had to be you. You are key.'

'And James is the vessel?'

'Eternal betrayed. Beaten. Hidden. Wants return. Will return. But needs body. This body,' he said, pointing to James.

'Oh, fuck no, Porky,' I replied.

'James the vessel. James born to hold the Father. You will open the door, set free, James will give The Eternal form. Life. He will live and walk among us again.'

He stopped by a door and opened it, we left Other London behind and walked towards Stonehenge.

'Listen mate,' I said, 'there is literally zero chance of any of that happening.'

'All is written.'

'I don't give a flying fuck. I'm not opening any door, and no dickless wonder is stuffing himself into my brother.'

'This the end. Always knew. I am ready.'

I whipped out the white-bladed knife and dragged it across the pig's throat. A great arterial gush flooded from his neck, and he fell to his knees, choking, gasping, then toppled forward, sending a delta of blood rippling between the cobbles.

'None of it is happening,' I cried. I looked around, but James was gone.

'Good, Erin,' said Scarbury, his red robes flapping in the midnight wind.

'Fuck you, pal,' I replied, running at him, knife white-knuckled in my fist.

I wasn't a pawn in someone's prophecy. Not me, not my brother.

'He's waiting for you,' said Scarbury.

He didn't try to get out of the way. Didn't try to fight back. Like the pig, he just took it, the blade sliding into his stomach, his hands grasping my forearm. Not to push me away, just a reflex.

'This knife. This knife was my end. Was our end. The knife with the blade of white.' I pulled it free and sunk it into his stomach again. Scarbury coughed and smiled, bright red blood dribbling from his mouth. 'Our part is played. Time to step off the stage. But not you. Not yet. Still a few pages left for you.'

'Shut up!'

I pulled the blade free again, blood splattering against my stomach, my thighs, and held it high above me, gripping the hilt with both hands.

Scarbury nodded blissfully. 'It has been my greatest honour. And now, I die.'

I screamed and brought the knife down hard, the blade splitting his skull in two. Scarbury shook, spasmed, his twin-sun eyes turning cold, and then he crumpled to the dirt, dead.

I staggered backwards, shaking, jubilant, my hands slick with blood.

'Come on, then,' I yelled at the sky. 'Face me!'

A wind blew and reality melted away.

I fell.

...

...

...

I hadn't liked the look in my brother's eyes.

26

I was sat in a chair in a room made of marble. The floor, the walls, the ceiling. Brilliant white stone streaked with veins of black. This was definitely better than when I'd opened my eyes and found myself floating in space and being chased by a one-eyed space whale. A comfy chair in a nice, temperate room is always better than drifting alone through the cosmos. Ask anyone.

'Well, this is awkward,' said Carlisle.

I turned to find two more chairs behind mine. In one sat Carlisle, in the other, Kirklander.

'Wait, how did we get here?' asked Kirk, sitting forward and looking around wildly as though he'd just that moment woken up.

I stood and rounded on Carlisle, who remained relaxed in his seat. 'You fucker,' I yelled.

'Potty mouth,' he replied.

Kirk stood and joined me. 'You betrayed us. I died because of you.'

'And yet you seem very much alive to me.'

'Give me one good reason why I shouldn't carve out your arsehole and use it for a cock ring,' Kirk demanded.

Carlisle smiled, his eyes dark. 'Feel free to try. I have no compunction against murdering you both, but right now I feel as though we have more pressing concerns. Such as how we came to be here, where "here" is, and who is that man lurking behind you, quietly watching us?'

I whirled around to find a man walking in our direction.

Not just any man.

James.

He was naked still, and walked with easy confidence, a happy look on his face.

'James...' I stepped forward, Kirk holding my wrist, pulling me back.

'Kirk, that's my brother.'

'Wait just a second.'

James stopped and looked at us all in turn. 'Friends. Welcome. It's been a long time since I've enjoyed company.'

Carlisle stood, flapping the tails of his coat out nonchalantly as he joined us. 'And just where is it that we are joining you?'

'My home. My prison.'

His eyes met mine. It was the same look I'd seen before I'd been spirited away from the room under Stonehenge. The look I didn't like. The one that made me so uneasy.

'James, it's me. It's Erin.'

He walked towards me and took my hand in his, still smiling. I felt an urge to pull away and run, but my legs wouldn't cooperate.

'You I love,' he said. 'All three of you, in fact. So important. I've dreamed of you all for so long. For centuries. This last hundred years I've been so eager for what is about to happen. I've been giddy. And now, at last, here we all are.'

It wasn't him.

'You three, at last, here. What a gift.'

It was and it wasn't. That realisation hit me with a clear certainty. It was and it wasn't him.

'What have you done with my brother?'

He let go of my hand and walked a circle around us, hands clasped behind his back. 'I'm here. I'm right here.'

'Erin, that is not your brother,' said Carlisle, keeping his distance.

'What the hell is going on?' asked Kirklander.

'You're not him. You are, but you aren't. What have you done to James?'

He stopped and leaned against one of the chairs. 'I have made him more. Much more. More than he would have ever been. It wasn't my choice, I want to make that clear. This is just how it was written. You know that, right?'

'So it was written that we three would journey to this place?' said Carlisle.

James smiled and nodded.

'My fate is my own,' said Carlisle, a steel edge entering his voice. 'Those who try to make me dance to their tune very swiftly find their bones crushed beneath my boot.'

James laughed and clapped his hands together. 'I do enjoy you, Carlisle. Always have. All the things you've done over your long and wicked life. That business in Blackpool with the imprisoned angel. Riveting stuff. Saw a bit of myself in him, I did.'

Carlisle pulled a knife and tossed it with speed and accuracy. The knife melted into butter two feet from James.

'Please, this is a time for celebration, not fighting. We are all part of something greater than ourselves here. Can't you feel it?'

'Who are you?' asked Kirk.

'You know who I am. I am The Eternal. Where I walk I leave pain, I leave death, and blah blah blah. I'm sure you've heard all this sort of stuff before. Drink?'

A trolley laden with crystal decanters appeared by his side. He lifted a glass and poured himself two fingers of whisky.

'I remember you, Erin. Specific memories of our past together. Not long memories. Fragments, really. Remnants that have been left behind, rattling around in my head. I can see you looking down at me in my crib. I can hear you reading to me. I can hear scraps of songs that you sang to me as I drifted off to sleep.'

'I'll ask you one more time,' I said, anger bubbling like magma, 'what have you done with my brother?'

He swallowed his drink and sighed. 'Look. Your brother was born for one reason and one reason alone. To be a vessel. To be *my* vessel. We took him so that the two of us could bond, slowly, over the years. So that when the time came for you three to enter the story again, he'd be ready. I slipped inside and scooped out all that was him so all that was left was me.'

He was dead. James was dead, that's what he was saying. He'd trapped him, fed him, allowed him to grow until he was ready to step inside, then thrown away anything that was left of my brother. He just wanted his flesh, his bones, his brain. He'd done all that, hollowed James out and worn him like a human suit, all because of some so-called prophecy. Some fucking story. The physical body that my baby brother grew to be was looking at me, but James was long gone.

'Afraid so,' replied The Eternal. Not James, The Eternal, reading my thoughts. 'Again, if it's any consolation, it's not like he had a choice. Or me for that matter. We're all just acting out a story that was written a long time ago.'

'I'm going to kill you. I promise,' I said out loud.

'Do not be foolish,' said Carlisle. 'Why do you think this thing is known as The Eternal?'

'He's right, Erin,' said The Eternal, a look on his face like he was almost sad to crush my hopes. 'I am The Eternal. Even if I wanted to die I couldn't. You think if I could be killed that an army of witches and wizards wouldn't have finished the job instead of locking me up here?'

'Fuck this,' said Kirk, 'we can have a go.'

He grunted and threw a wall of crackling purple magic towards The Eternal. It rippled and warped and turned into a cloud of songbirds that whirled around The Eternal before sweeping away into the shadows.

'Elric Cuthbert Kirklander,' said The Eternal, giving him a strange, fey look. 'The changes you've made over the years... I won't pretend I don't feel a little proud of you. My boy's all grown up.'

'I really dislike this guy,' said Kirk. 'Even more than I dislike you, pasty, and about half an hour ago you murdered me.'

Carlisle turned to him, curious. 'How did you escape that fate? I expected the Long Man to be admiring your screaming soul by now.'

'You knew about that?' I asked.

'Of course. I told you. When I looked into him I saw nothing. I was being a touch oblique, perhaps, but I meant that I could see his soul was no longer his own. I look at you now and see that you too are empty.'

The Eternal pushed the drinks trolley towards us and poured four glasses. We all took one as he raised his in a toast. 'To you three. My saviours. The soulless trio.'

He drank.

'Wait, soulless *trio*?' I said.

Carlisle tossed his drink back but said nothing.

'Carlisle here lost ownership of his soul long before you two, isn't that right?'

'I may have acted rather rashly during that fallen angel business, and promised my eternal spark to a demon known as the Yellow Man. And all in the name of doing the right thing.' He grimaced like he had a terrible taste in his mouth, despite the whisky being perfect. 'That's where helping others gets you. Far better to be selfish.' He poured himself a second glass.

'You reverted to type in the end,' said The Eternal, flopping down on one of the chairs, quite relaxed.

'I take it there will be no offers of riches and power?' asked Carlisle.

'Afraid not. That was an embellishment. It's an old story, people like to add bits in the retelling. Sorry.'

Carlisle lifted his glass and nodded his head. 'Fuck you.'

He drank as The Eternal laughed.

'Wait, why is that important?' I said. 'Why is none of us having souls such a big deal?'

'Because it's what's written,' replied The Eternal. 'You, Erin Banks, assassin, will turn the key. Even now I'm reaching a hand into your world, but it will take three without souls to push the door open wide enough for me to step through fully. To finally get out of this place. Let me tell you, I've been going stir crazy cooped up in here. It'll be nice to get out and stretch the old legs.'

'I'm starting to think selling my soul might have been a mistake,' said Kirklander.

We'd all been played. All been given just enough to keep us walking towards this place. To make us act out the story that he and Scarbury and that fucking pig were so enamoured with.

My brother was dead and I didn't know what to do. All those years he'd been alive, waiting for me. Maybe if I'd found him earlier I'd have been able to get him out of this. Save him. Save him before The Eternal took full control, before he ejected everything that was James. But I didn't. I'd let him down again, too busy living my stupid life, distracted, when I should have been tearing the world down looking for him.

Too late.

Too late.

James was dead, and now a monster was looking at me through his eyes, smiling and chatting.

Carlisle placed his glass down. I drank mine, then Kirk's.

'Well, this has been some extremely illuminating stuff,' said Carlisle. 'But I think it is about time we called it a night.'

'Of course,' replied The Eternal. 'This is the bit where you run.'

We turned and ran. Our boots echoed loudly as they pounded against the room's marble floor. A room that seemed to stretch on forever, with no walls, no doors, no exit in sight.

He didn't chase us.

'This is the bit where you run.'

Fuck.

Fuck fucking fuck.

Even this bit he knew. He knew and he told us and we were doing it anyway. Like we couldn't *not* do it, even though we knew we shouldn't. All three of us must have been thinking the same. We should do anything but run. Hop on the spot or lay down or twirl in circles, anything but run away, because that's what he said we should do. What the story said we should do.

But we ran anyway.

'Is there a part two to this amazing plan?' asked Kirklander.

'I think part two might be "we're buggered". Is it?' I said.

'You both have the memory of a goldfish,' said Carlisle.

'Great, insults from the backstabber,' said Kirk.

'None of us is pure, fool,' said Carlisle.

'What have we forgotten?' I asked.

'I told you both. One of my abilities is to create exit points. Wherever we are, if I have enough time, I can figure out how to weave together an escape hatch.'

'Well, good,' said Kirklander. 'That's good, right?'

'What if this is it?' I asked. 'He said we open the door for him. What if this is you opening that door?'

'No. The doors I create open for only those I wish them to.'

We stopped running and looked back. The Eternal hadn't followed us.

'You sure about that?' I asked.

Carlisle paused. 'No.'

'Great,' I replied. 'Really, really double-great.'

'Okay,' said Carlisle, 'I needed space and time. This should be enough.'

He dropped down into a cross-legged position on the ground, his eyes closed.

'Now is not the time for a power nap,' said Kirk, looking around wildly.

I could feel what he was feeling. We were being watched. The room was growing darker at the edges. Something was closing in on us.

'Don't go,' came The Eternal's voice. I whirled around,

fists clenched, tattoos like ice, but I couldn't find him. It was like he was speaking directly into my ear, but I couldn't see the man speaking.

'Hurry up,' I said, my voice a whisper.

I could feel it again. The new, dark power begging to be unleashed. I didn't know what would happen if I did.

I thought about what Parker had told me during the Liyta case. I wasn't built to handle too much magic. It could destroy me. That's why the half-human Liyta had died. Her magic wore her down until there was nothing left. What would this dark magic do to me?

Tendrils of black were weaving out of the shadows towards us. Or maybe the shadows themselves were reaching out.

'Hurry,' yelled Kirk, his fists blazing with magic.

Carlisle didn't answer, didn't open his eyes. Instead, he stayed sat in a half lotus position with a look of serene blankness on his face, as though he were taking a Sunday afternoon yoga class.

A spark.

A crackle of static.

Something was forming in front of Carlisle.

'He's doing it,' said Kirk, unleashing ball after ball of magic into the black to seemingly no effect. 'He is, isn't he?'

I didn't answer.

The darkness pressed in. It was eight steps away from us, seven, six. It was death. An endless wave of death, ready to crash against us, against everything.

'Any time now,' yelled Kirk, his perfect hair in disarray, sticking to his sweaty face in clumps.

He fired off more and more magic, but he might as well have been throwing cotton balls at a charging bull.

'Carlisle,' I said, crouching at his side, 'it's time to go.'

He opened an eye and smiled. 'Now.'

The spark, the static, a door formed. Carlisle jumped through. I grabbed Kirklander's wrist and pulled him towards the light and...

...

...

I gasped, sitting bolt upright. I was back in the chamber under Stonehenge. A gasp to my right, my left, Kirklander and Carlisle.

Normally at this point you'd celebrate, but we had nothing to cheer. Surrounding us was the masked crowd.

'Out of the frying pan,' said Carlisle.

He and Kirklander stood back-to-back, unleashing fire on the crowd that surrounded us. The mob didn't run or scream. Instead, they clapped and cheered and laughed. They were happy. Happy even as their bodies were pummelled and destroyed.

I turned to the column of light at the centre of the room. James' body still hung inside. His eyes were open and he was smiling. He lifted his hands and pressed against the edge of the light. Black cracks began to spread across it from his fingers. The light was breaking.

'We have to stop the key from turning,' I screamed.

Kirk looked over his shoulder at The Eternal. The base stone with all ten keys inserted inside it was turning. Slowly. Inch by inch. As it rotated, more black cracks appeared in the column of light holding The Eternal's vessel. Holding my brother's body.

Carlisle unleashed a rope of fierce, molten magic that encircled the stone like a lasso. He gripped the rope, wrapped it around his wrist, and leaned back, the heels of his boots digging into the floor, the veins on his neck bulging as he tried to halt the stone's motion. Kirklander sent a surge of bright purple magic through the lasso that attacked the stone. The stone slowed, even crumbled a little, but it wasn't stopping. The key was still turning in the lock.

He was going to escape. The Eternal was going to cross over.

'You have to do it now,' said Carlisle, shaking with effort.

'Do what?'

'You know what.'

'I don't!'

'The Long Man gave you a gift. I can see it in you. Use it.'

I flexed my hands and my tattoos bloomed electric blue. 'I'm not like you,' I said.

'I know. Because you'll risk yourself to help others.'

'I'm an assassin.'

'But not in your heart. I know myself when I see it, and you are not me.'

'Fuck,' yelled Kirklander. 'It's not working, it's not working.'

My tattoos grew a darker shade of blue. I shivered, but not because I was cold.

'Do it,' said Carlisle. 'He gave you access to a dark, terrible, hungry magic. Yes, it might destroy you, but think of your brother. He deserves revenge, yes?'

I looked to Carlisle and tasted death in my mouth, sharp and sour. 'Yes.'

'You owe him that. Whatever the price.'

He was just trying to make me do what he wanted. I knew that. I also knew he was right.

Revenge.

At last.

I had no choice, I didn't.

I had to do this, for James.

For my parents.

For me.

'Let it off the leash,' cried Carlisle, blood dripping from his eyes, his nose.

The key was turning. The mob were cheering, dancing, wild. I placed my fists together as the ice spread, my tattoos burning brighter than ever.

It was going to shred the flesh from my bones.

It would kill me.

But I'd kill him.

I'd kill the thing that took my brother and destroyed my family. I could hear it, the magic. Voices upon voices. They weren't words I could understand, if they were words at all. The voices were unhinged, desperate, a chorus of destruction. They begged me to let them go, building and building and building. I was a dam, and at any moment a crack was going to appear, and the whole thing would come crashing down.

'Erin,' said Kirklander. He sounded like he was a long way away. 'Erin, what's wrong with your eyes?'

I looked up at the body that used to be my brother. At The Eternal, a creature that had scooped him out and thrown away his innards like the brains of a Halloween pumpkin.

'I am free,' he said, pressing against the light.

The dark in me knew he was wrong.

'No.'

The Eternal's brow creased as he looked at me. 'What are you doing?'

Didn't he know? Maybe this wasn't how it was written. Maybe, in the end, I'd gone off script. I wondered. The black magic in me, ancient magic born in Hell, screamed to be allowed out. I couldn't hold it back any more.

I had to let go. Let go of the magic. Of my own life?

'Do it,' urged Carlisle.

I let out a breath and looked at the thing that had once been my brother.

'Fuck you.'

And then I let the dark loose.

27

I t almost killed me. *Almost* being the operative word.

Yeah, I lived. I'm not exactly sure what happened after the black magic erupted from me. Kirklander couldn't say for sure. All he could tell me was that it was like watching a volcano erupt. A volcano full of the universe's bile.

With Carlisle's help, we escaped, back above ground to Stonehenge itself. I don't remember that part. Why didn't it kill me? It should have done. I'd seen what could happen if someone like me abused magic. Magic bigger than we could handle. It should have torn me apart. What exactly had the Long Man done to me?

Weeks passed, months, and the magic didn't wear off, though I was mostly too scared to use it. It seemed like the power was always there, prowling inside a cage night and day, ready for me to pop open the gate.

The Eternal was stopped. I think. Carlisle kept watch on Stonehenge for the next six months. Employed the eaves' network to search for any word, any hint, that The Eternal was walking the Earth again. So far, they'd come up with nothing. He didn't do that for us, or the rest of the world. I'm pretty sure he did it for himself. He'd be high on The Eternal's shit list if he was still around, so he'd best watch his back.

The first time I'd seen Carlisle, after I recovered from my dark magic volcano showcase, I'd punched him right in his pasty fucking face. Twice. Broke his nose and split his bottom lip in half. 'That's for trying to fuck us over, and that's for killing Kirk.'

He didn't hit me back, or worse. Instead, he smiled, dabbed the blood from his face, bowed slightly, and walked away.

James was dead, but I'd avenged him. I think. I didn't like the uncertainty, but it was all I had. Until I knew any different, I was going to assume his killer had been stopped. Yeah, not ideal, but what else was I gonna do?

No, I didn't tell my parents. They wouldn't have believed me anyway. I'd done all of this partly for them, but it didn't change things. We were broken and we weren't gonna be fixed.

So what now?

Same old same old. Well, more or less.

I leaned back in my chair and swung my boots up on the desk. Kirklander stuck his head around the door of our office. Yeah, an office. *Our* office.

'Hey there, beautiful,' he said, wearing a smile that could moisten knickers at twenty paces.

'How'd it go?'

He raised a bloody duffel bag. 'We landed a rush order. Two heads, one big pay day.'

He tossed the goods into the corner of the room. 'Where's my cut?'

'It's already in our account,' I said.

Again with the *our*. I know.

The office we were inhabiting was what used to be Black Cat Ink. It turned out Parker had owned the premises outright, and was kind enough to leave it to me in his will. Now I worked out of it. Well, we did. Me and Kirk. Uncannies For Hire.

I stood and walked over to him, wrapping my arms around his neck and pulling his face down so I could plant a kiss on him.

We were together.

Together together.

Not just in business, but, you know, mushy boyfriend-girlfriend, lovey-dovey stuff, too. I know, don't you just hate a sappy ending?

The upstairs door opened and a visitor arrived. 'Yeesh,' said Cupid, catching me and Kirk going at it, 'if we had an H.R. department, I'd be lodging a complaint.'

I pulled away from Kirk and gave Cupid the middle finger. Yeah, he was on the payroll, too. And I let him sleep at the office, as well. No more hanging out by the pier.

Cupes flopped down on the couch, the same couch that had been there when Parker ran the place, and plucked a half-smoked cigar from his nappy.

'One for me, fatso?' said Kirk.

Cupid grimaced, then tossed one his way. Kirk caught it and joined him on the couch. No one swore. No one threatened violence. I think they were starting to like each other.

'Ow! Hey! The little fucker burned me!' said Kirk, as Cupid started laughing.

Okay, maybe we had a little way to go.

I twirled in my chair. I'd had the recliner I used to sit in when Parker tattooed me repurposed into office furniture. I gripped the chair's soft leather arms and smiled.

'You done good, girl.'

'Thanks, Parks.'

'What's that?' asked Kirk.

'Just talking to a dead man in my imagination again,' I replied.

He shook his head and smiled. 'Why is it always the crazy ones?' He inhaled his cigar and blew out a thick lance of blue smoke.

I'd done it.

We'd done it.

Uncovered it all.

Killed the bad guy.

At last.

I think.

Christ, I hoped so.

So what next?

I looked over at Kirklander again. He was smiling at me. I liked what I saw in his eyes.

Next? Everything.

The End.

LEAVE A REVIEW

Reviews are gold to indie authors, so if you've enjoyed this book, please consider visiting the site you purchased it from and leaving a quick review.

BECOME AN INSIDER

Sign up and receive **FREE UNCANNY KINGDOM BOOKS**. Also, be the **FIRST** to hear about **NEW RELEASES** and **SPECIAL OFFERS** in the **UNCANNY KINGDOM** universe. Just visit:

WWW.UNCANNYKINGDOM.COM

MORE STORIES SET IN THE UNCANNY KINGDOM

The Hexed Detective Series
Hexed Detective
Fatal Moon
Night Terrors

The Branded Series
Sanctified
Turned
Bloodline

The London Coven Series
Familiar Magic
Nightmare Realm
Deadly Portent

The Spectral Detective Series
Spectral Detective
Corpse Reviver
Twice Damned

The Dark Lakes Series
Magic Eater
Blood Stones
Past Sins

16355888R00139

Printed in Great Britain
by Amazon